THE
ACTION
OF
THE
TIGER

 AN INNER SANCTUM MYSTERY

Thomas
Walsh

Simon and Schuster
New York

Then imitate the action of the tiger:

Stiffen the sinews, summon up the blood,

Disguise fair nature with hard-favour'd rage;

Then lend the eye a terrible aspect . . .

King Henry V, III, 1

The Action of the Tiger

CHAPTER *1*

It was Christina Elizabeth Dillon to the last inch. The first week, a bit homesick apparently, she wrote almost every afternoon to her brother Johnny, and called him several times long distance. The second week, much more acclimated by then, she settled for one very brief note and a single picture postcard with her initials scrawled on it. But for the third week, day after day, there was nothing at all, not to anyone in the family, not one line.

And yet she was very much annoyed when he called her person to person up there in Hazard Lake on the second Friday in July. Perhaps she was still a child, she informed him loftily; an infant in arms. Perhaps she should write to him twice a day now, morning and evening. Was that it? But how old did he imagine she was, anyway? Could he remember?

And he could remember. That was exactly the point for Dillon. She had been sixteen last March. But he knew better than to resent or command her, because more and more these days it was Chrissy who managed and supervised him, and with very little nonsense about it. He placated her as usual therefore. It was, Dillon explained feebly, her sister Loretta who had been getting a bit worried the past day or two; not him. But what was the matter up there, anyway? She had promised to write home at least twice a week. She had promised faithfully.

"Oh, for cream's sake!" she exclaimed, as if altogether out of patience with him. "Worried! Then go ahead. Keep checking on me. I simply haven't the slightest idea of how to look out for myself. Is that it?"

Perhaps it was. Sixteen, Dillon had been reminding himself uneasily this past week; away from home for the first time; and not half so poised and sophisticated as she liked to pretend with people. He hedged feebly again.

"Well, you know Loretta," he said. "She keeps saying that I should never have let you take the job up there. Rita, too. I'm getting it thrown at me from all sides, Chris. You don't know. Do you need anything, though? Did you forget anything?"

Which proved to be reasonably solid ground for him. She usually did forget something. She had this time.

"Dear, darling Loretta," she said. Her tone withered; but then Loretta, who was her oldest sister, had always been a much more difficult proposition for Chris than Dillon himself. "Oh, sweet. But if she calls again about me, you might try telling her to mind her own business for once. I like the nerve. And I suppose you could send me . . . let's see now. There's a black leather belt in one of my bureau drawers somewhere, or in the closet.

Just look around for it. And my yellow bathrobe, too, and my new tennis racket, and that cashmere sweater you gave me last Christmas. Now be sure and send all those things special delivery, Johnny. Sometimes it's a little cool here when I get up. I really need them."

"Nothing else?" Dillon asked her. "You sure now?"

But irony was never a useful weapon with her. She had thoughts that ran in their own uncomplicated and direct fashion, to whatever it was Chrissy wanted, with no subtleties permitted.

"Well, I don't think so," she announced, after deliberating about it. "Or maybe those brown-and-white shoes, if you can find them anywhere, and a box of chocolate cherries from that place over on Lexington Avenue; a big box. You just can't get them up here. But you want to hear something, Johnny? I'm getting filthy rich. Can you imagine? I made sixty-four dollars and eighty cents in tips this week, and I'm writing it all down in a little notebook I got; every penny. I'm keeping strict count."

She was a great one, Dillon remembered, for strict count. The only trouble was that each improved bookkeeping system lasted about three days; then financial chaos again.

"You do that," he advised her. "Very good, Chris. Or see if you can't get hold of a certified public accountant for yourself. How's the weather up there?"

"You wouldn't believe it," she said. "Not in July. It's just perfect. Peg and I went swimming this afternoon. You see one day we're on from noon to six at the drive-in, and the next from six until closing time. First we get like Monday afternoon off, and then Tuesday evening. You see what I mean?"

"Now that's right," Dillon said. "You do, don't you? Glad you explained it to me. You're not still homesick, are you?"

"Oh, crying my eyes out. Homesick!" But perhaps the suggestion was not so ridiculous as all that. It seemed to him that her tone softened. "Gosh, I miss you," she said. "Honest. Or all the grouching and bossing I used to get. I do, Johnny. I must be crazy. Why don't you drive up next weekend?"

"We'll see," Dillon told her; but he had only been waiting for Chris to make the suggestion herself, before he had to. "Maybe I will. Now what did you say you wanted up there? The belt and the brown shoes and what else, Chris?"

That time First Grade Detective John Patrick Dillon made a list of everything, several additional items having been thought of in the meantime, and mailed off her package as soon as possible the next day. Then later on, after the usual full day at his midtown precinct house, he picked up his girl, Rita Nielsen, in Rockaway Beach, and drove her to his sister Margaret's in Flatbush for Saturday night dinner.

There the ordinary quota of small chores was waiting for him. He put on a new screen door, rewired one of the living-room lamps, fixed a wheel on the baby carriage and patched two leaks in the washer hose. "But what surprises me," he confided to Rita afterward, when they were out in the car, "is how that fellow she married can even manage to tie his own shoelaces in the morning. There's a clown, all right, if I ever saw one."

"Well, she likes him," Rita said. "And he was her own free choice, wasn't he?" She was way over in the front seat from him, a bad sign, because Dillon had certain plans for the evening. It was why he had contrived to leave Meg's place a bit early. "What would she need a handyman in the house for, with brother Johnny around? Don't forget that next time you're expected to do over the downstairs hall for them. Bring your own

12

paint, too. But you didn't catch any of those delicate little hints that were floating around?"

"What?" Dillon said. He had been wondering absently if he couldn't manage the hall next Wednesday night, maybe, if he got off from the precinct a bit early. "Now come on," he began persuading her. "What are you fussing about? It's still only ten o'clock, Rita. I thought it was a lot later, somehow. You want to go home this early?"

"Right straight ahead on the parkway," Rita said. "If you care to bother, that is. Yes, I do." And she remained way over on her side of the car, looking crisp and attractive in a short-sleeved white dress with a gracefully becoming flare to the skirt. But then she was always very stylish, his sister Meg thought, so that everything she made must go on her back, if Meg knew anything at all about what clothes cost these days; and very high and mighty, too, all of a sudden very standoffish and snappy with other people.

"Wow!" Dillon said, attempting a manner of good-humored playfulness with her. "Straight home, eh? Okay, then; whatever you want, of course. But what's the matter, hon? Do you have a headache or something?"

"Or something," Rita said. "That's it. No fussing from me tonight about anything at all; but no tender and loving suggestions from you, either. That's fair enough, wouldn't you think?"

Then she knew, Dillon understood. He had an idea that he might have colored the least bit; and yet, with a touchy masculine resentment also in evidence, it seemed necessary to make her admit that she did know.

"Suggestions about what?" he demanded, with hypocritical innocence. "I don't like that remark. Suppose somebody else heard it, eh? It wouldn't sound right."

"Wouldn't it?" Rita said. The white dress had always just suited her, from Dillon's viewpoint. It set off her crisp blond hair, the dark and intense blue eyes and the smoothly flowing feminine lines of bust and shoulders. She was a tall, slender girl with a superb carriage, and his heart had ached a little all night, watching her. It ached now.

"Then maybe," she said, still keeping herself carefully out of contact with him, "maybe it doesn't feel right, either; not any more. But let's not get into another hassle about ourselves, Johnny. I'm not in the mood. Just take me straight home, will you?"

"Whatever you want," he repeated grimly. But it was a matter of stubborn masculine pride now. He had to go on with it. "Only what did that crack about loving little suggestions mean? You mind telling me?"

"I don't believe so," Rita said. "Suggestion one, then. Let's stop off for a nice, quiet drink somewhere, because it's still early. Suggestion two. Let's stop off at your apartment for a half hour, and you could make some of those rum punches I like. And that would be perfectly all right, of course. We wouldn't have to worry about Chrissy catching us; she's away for the whole rest of the summer now. It all appears to have been very neatly arranged, doesn't it?"

"Now I told you before!" Dillon exploded at her. He was thirty-one, five or six years older than Rita, thin and wiry, but perhaps a little too finely drawn in physical build. He had a nervous stomach, edgy mannerisms, hot brown eyes, very dark red hair—and the legendary temper associated with such coloring. "You seem to be getting pretty smart these days, Rita; pretty smart. But watch your step. I don't want you talking like that, and I'm telling you for the last time. What's the matter, anyway?"

But he knew what the matter was. In a certain reluctant way, he even shared her feeling about it. The difference between them was that he had no desire to discuss the problem in cold blood. Women, he told himself. God Almighty! Always something.

"Well, I might be a lot of things," Rita said, her expression remaining hard as a stone against him, "but I don't think you could describe me as pretty smart, Johnny. I wish I had been. I mean when you drove me up to the Catskills this spring, and my cousin Louise wasn't home; when we took two rooms in town at that elegant new motel, and used one; when we finally plighted our troth to one another, since I imagine you'd prefer to think of it in that way. No, don't interrupt me again. Let me quite finish, please. I want you to know that I'm fed up to the ears with this whole thing that's going on between us, and ashamed of myself, and bitterly disgusted. So disgusted that I wouldn't care one snap of my fingers if— But what's the use talking about it? Take me home, Johnny. I told Mamma I'd probably be in early. Just do me the favor."

It was by now the old and only too familiar accusation between them. He set his teeth.

"Then go ahead," he declared. "Say anything you want to me. Keep talking and talking about it, if it makes you feel any better. But maybe I don't care a hell of a lot, either, what happens; not if we have to go on arguing like this. I thought we were two people pretty much in love with each other, and that we had all our plans made to get married next June. But if we aren't—"

"Oh, I know," Rita said, with a cold, bitter look for him this time, a cold, bitter tone. "How shameless and despicable to even mention it. How low, really. Well, I intend to mention it, anyway. Why did you send Chrissy up to the mountains this summer? And answer me that one question, if you can answer. You wanted to get rid of her, didn't you, so that we'd have the apartment to ourselves, and that whenever the mood struck you . . . That's the truth of it, and you know it is. You managed the whole thing."

It was such an unjust and unfounded declaration against him that it literally staggered Dillon. He had trouble collecting himself.

"You think that?" he demanded. "You believe I deliberately— Now listen here, Rita. I've taken a lot from you lately. But if you imagine I'm going to sit here and listen to stuff like that . . ."

She remained very calm.

"Then drop me off at the next stop," she said. "That's simple enough. Don't listen to it. Only admit the truth, why don't you? That you deliberately arranged this thing about Chrissy. Try to be some kind of man, Johnny Dillon."

And now he was beginning to understand that this was something Rita believed of him, actually; only how could she believe it? The idea was insane, Dillon knew. He had to keep protesting about it.

"But you know we had it all arranged," he began anxiously. "I had to get Chris through high school first; then, when Loretta bought her new house out in Bayside, she'd move in with them; and after that we'd get married right away. You want us to set the date here and now? Is that it? Then go ahead. Any time you say, Rita. Just name it."

"Just name it yourself," Rita said, the blue eyes flashing contemptuously around at him. "So you're ready to do the decent thing, are you? The great concession. You'll actually marry the girl. But of course after Chrissy gets out of high school next year. After that. And in the meanwhile, since you've got this whole lovely summer in front of you, we can make a regular Saturday engagement of it. Well, you can just think again about that part. It isn't going to wash in the same dirty tub any more. It might have taken me quite a while to find out something silly and old-fashioned about myself, but I have, finally. I'm not that kind of girl, that's all. I never was."

So they had come to the brick wall again. Always that stupid feminine resentment of poor little Chris, Dillon told himself; or of Loretta, or Margaret, or Agnes; always one or the other of the Dillon sisters to throw in his face; always the same thing. He gave another grim nod.

"And I suppose I never told you," he said. "Never. Not a word. I never explained to you the first month we started going together how I had to look out for the whole bunch of them after Mamma died twelve years ago. Who else did they have? I told you right off the spot I was in, how I promised Mamma. I told you and told you. I'm tired telling you."

"And maybe I'm tired hearing it," Rita said, her voice beginning to shake oddly; but no tears, however, not from Rita. "It's always those sisters of yours above everyone else, and then me, maybe. Little Chrissy, for instance—your own sweet precious. When that young imp makes a complete fool out of you. When any time she wants to, she can twist you around her finger in two seconds. But you won't see that, either, or else you can't. You spoil her rotten, that's all, and you always have, everyone in the family outside of Loretta. Chrissy the baby!"

"So that's it," Dillon said, lighting a cigarette blindly, and just missing a station wagon in the next lane. "Blame Chris for everything; a kid like that. You ought to feel real proud of yourself, Rita. I always thought you liked her a lot. That's what you made out, any-way."

It proved to be a very cunning touch on his part,

without intention, however; immediately effective. She flushed up.

"I didn't mean that," she protested angrily. "And you know I didn't. Stop twisting things! But Loretta warned you that she was a lot too young and unsophisticated to go up there and take a car-hopping job, and I warned you. Would you listen to us? And the crazy way you let her fix herself up, too; eye shadow all over, and nothing less than a beehive hairdo for her. She should have had her face smacked. But you knew what you were doing, all right. Get Chris out of the way, and then I could call Mamma any night you wanted, and tell her I was staying in town again with Grace Conklin. And what do you think that makes me, Johnny Dillon? How do you suppose I feel when I know the idea in your head? Take just one wild guess about it, if you want to, and then drop me off at the next corner. I can find a cab for myself. Let me out of this car."

"You're going to sit right where you are," Dillon warned her, a bit pale suddenly. "Now I'm telling you, Rita. We can get the license first thing Monday morning, if that's what you want. Only why can't we wait until we have Chris settled? What's the rush, all of a sudden? Use your head, can't you?"

"Why, no rush at all," Rita said, but in a tone that made him understand it was the last fatal suggestion from his side. "Obviously. We've got a nice sleazy little affair going. Why spoil it? But are you going to let me out of this car now? Are you?"

He lost his temper again. It was becoming intolerable for him.

"Then what the hell do you want me to do?" he almost shouted at her. "Just tell me. You don't understand it yourself, that's what. You know I love you. You know I never looked at another girl in my life. And still—"

After that it plunged altogether out of their control, as it often did lately; accusation and counteraccusation, bitterness, hurtful and angry words. Ten minutes later, when they parted at the Nielsens' house in Rockaway Beach, they were still at white heat, and she was out of the car seconds before Dillon could manage to get around and open the door for her.

It was by far their worst quarrel. He would not forget it, Dillon promised himself. But how was it possible that she could believe such a thing about him? It was simply not true, and he knew it wasn't. He would never in this world have let Chris go up there to Hazard Lake in the Adirondacks for his own reasons. That was a lie.

In fact, he had let her go only after she had kept nagging and nagging at him—night after night of tears, tempers, tantrums. He never wanted her to do anything, Chris had sobbed brokenly. He had everybody she knew laughing themselves sick at Chris Dillon. But all right. If her own brother hated her that much, then she hated him, too. She'd kill herself. Then he'd be sorry. She'd run away. Because why couldn't she go? Peg Riley would be with her, and he knew Peg, and they had it all fixed to live up there with Peg's uncle and aunt, who ran the drive-in. So she didn't care what he said. She was going, anyway. Why couldn't she have a swell summer for herself, and make some money? Why couldn't she? Then more tears and tantrums, more broken sobs, banged doors, hating silences. Until in the end . . .

So by the time he got home his stomach was knotting up in quite the usual fashion; lumps in there hard as unripe crab apples. And suppose it was true, what Rita said? Suppose he had let Chris take the job up there so that he could have the apartment to himself all summer? It was certainly true that she had warned him against the thing, and so had Loretta. Even Mamma had warned him.

"Now Lorry will help you," Mamma had whispered that last day in the hospital, twelve years ago, with the sticky sweetness of the oxygen tent around them. There were times when Dillon could still smell that. He began smelling it now, in his apartment kitchen. "She's got a sound, sensible head on her shoulders, Johnny. I think even Margaret and Agnes will try their best if anything happens to me here, and small as they are. But Chris, there's the one. She wants her own way, and I'm afraid that we've all babied her too much. So remember that, and keep a firm hand on her, Johnny. She'll need it. I know it's a hard promise I'm asking from you, to look out for them now, but I could die easy if you gave it to me. There'll be only you to keep them together, Johnny, with God's help. But remember about Chris, mind you. The firm hand with that one. Because if you don't—"

And he had promised, Dillon remembered. He had tried his best to look out for all of them ever since. For twelve years he had kept the family together, and paid for it, too. He had paid for it most of all, perhaps, with that lousy stomach of his, always worrying about one or the other of them, where they went, the fellows they knew, what time they got home.

There had been a day and a night job for him at least two or three years after Mamma died, and before he was even old enough to try for the department; but no girls. No time for them, no money, no inclination—or so Johnny Dillon had impressed stonily on himself. Yet he had never regretted that part. How could he? He had Rita now. He had always been pretty much of a loner before Rita, had to be; and maybe that had built up a little too much pressure in John Patrick Dillon over the years.

He made a pot of black coffee for himself. He understood what it was going to mean to that stomach of his; a bad night. But he seemed to want a bad night now; even deserved it, Dillon felt, because of course he could never forgive himself if anything happened to little Chris up there, just as he had never been able to forgive himself for what had happened to Eddie McManus.

Maybe, he decided wearily, worry about other people had become a conditioned reflex with him over the years. Rita might have known what she was talking about in that respect, anyway. But now and again he still felt that he should have gone up on the roof that night after those two hophead gunmen and left Eddie down in the yard. He would never have missed with his first shots up there, the way Eddie had; not Dillon the sharpshooter. Only of course he hadn't known exactly where the hopheads were, and Eddie hadn't. So how could he blame himself? But he remembered the feeling he'd had then, that some people weren't fit to live, even. It was probably a lucky thing for him that those fellows had been caught in another holdup a week later, because Johnny Dillon used to go out at three or four in the morning, sometimes, looking for them. And he wouldn't have arrested them, either; not after Eddie. He'd have . . .

The phone rang. It was five minutes past midnight—Sunday morning. He put down his cup quickly, everything eased and softened in him. He knew who it was—Rita. He could never have called her in a month of Sundays; something prevented; she had to call him. But that was the kind of girl she was; all anger and disdain with him one moment, all yielding and passionate tenderness with him the next moment. He did not, he felt suddenly and emotionally, deserve Rita; never would. But if they could only make up this thing between them . . .

"I was just coming in to call you myself," he lied to her. "I was, Rita. Couldn't sleep. All the way home I—"

Rita, however? There seemed to be a good deal of confusion on the other end of the line, a lot of voices in the background, and then a deep, masculine one cutting in stolidly. It wanted to know if this was a member of Miss Christina Dillon's immediate family on the line, and then it went on to something about a very serious accident.

Chris? Dillon thought. He stood motionless, holding the phone, but then turned quickly, and looked over at her picture on the mantel. What the the hell kind of a joke . . .

"Who's on here?" he demanded then. "Who is this?"

And it developed that a Chief Rutherfurd of the Hazard Lake Police Department was on here; no question. He stood motionless again. But a very serious accident, he understood, was the timeworn professional phrase, smoothing the road first, preparing somewhat. Often and often Detective Dillon had used it on similar occasions. So he understood at the first instant, actually, without quite believing it yet, that the something had happened up there. He knew that it must have happened. He knew Chrissy was dead.

CHAPTER *2*

But all they could tell him on the Saturday night was that it must have been a hit-and-run accident; not many details yet. They said that they had found her lying by the state highway up there at twenty minutes past eleven. And so three days later, next to Mamma, little Chris was buried in the Gate of Heaven Cemetery, just north of White Plains.

It was a heavy and listless July morning, brutally humid, and to Dillon the flowers piled up at each end of the mahogany casket gave a bewilderingly cheerful effect of color and bright gaiety. The fortunate thing was that Rita kept with him. He had no idea how he could have managed the thing without Rita; not possible. Even at the graveside she had to explain to other people what had happened, because Dillon himself still felt completely unable to give any account of the thing, whatever question was asked. He stood beside her then, listening painfully to what was said, and watching the funeral wreaths; but it did not seem to him that he was any part of the thing, and so much so that Rita had to get him started away when it was all over, when old Father Shaughnessy, from the Dillons' home parish up in the Bronx, had offered the last prayers. He would have done anything he was told by that time, obeyed anyone. Very often he did not realize that the other people were just two or three feet away, talking to him.

Back in the apartment there were sandwiches and iced tea waiting, prepared by old Mrs. Foley from the second floor. It was very hot in the apartment, also. Two or three electric fans hummed drearily in the living room, and all the windows were open. Chris's picture was still on the mantel. Her phonograph was beside the couch. Her records and movie magazines were piled in one corner.

The other people ate and drank, Dillon's brother-in-law Joe Farrell urging them; murmured condolences to Dillon; shook his hand; and went out. Rita sat down with him and asked quietly what he was doing with the records. He did not know. He just appeared to be sorting them out time after time, in an extremely careful manner, as if he wanted to find one in particular. But which one, exactly? He did not know that, either. But he was still doing it when other people came in, who had not heard about the funeral in time, and when Rita had to explain about the accident to them.

He got up then, standing as close as possible to Rita in his blue suit, white shirt and black tie. He looked thin and pale, eyes delicately shadowed around the lids as if by physical illness, and he listened to everything that was said with his head down, and an expression of hot, shiny restlessness on his face. Then at one o'clock, in order to get away by himself, he went downstairs for another carton of cigarettes from the corner drugstore.

When he came back that time it was much better. Only the family was left—Rita, the three surviving Dillon sisters and their husbands, and blond little Peg Riley, Chris's friend, with her mother and father. They were all talking when he opened the apartment door. They were all silent the moment he closed it. It was such a sudden and obvious constraint that it became apparent to him. He glanced helplessly at Rita.

"What is it?" he asked her. "What's the matter?"

"Nothing," Loretta told him. She was a little too sharp and too quick, however, as she always was when she had something worrying her. "It's all right. But come over here and sit down, Johnny, next to me. You look terrible. Didn't you sleep at all last night? Haven't you eaten anything?"

Then Joe Farrell came in from the kitchen, big cigar in mouth, another bottle of Scotch in his hand; drinks for everyone. He was Meg's husband, and he had got a little smart with her on their second or third date, so that she came home crying about it; but he never did that again. He and Johnny Dillon had had a quiet personal interview the next night, and after that things had been perfectly understood between them. They were still understood. They knew they despised each other.

"Little Chris," Farrell announced now, putting the whiskey down, and then solemnly and emotionally placing his hands on Dillon's shoulders. "I know how it is, John. Believe me. If that kid had been my own sister, I couldn't feel any worse about this. Little Chris."

"Now, Joe," Loretta said. She had always shared Dillon's opinion of him. "Joe."

"But I think he's got to be told," Farrell insisted. "And the sooner the better, Lorry. What the hell—we

25

don't know yet what they might be trying to pull up there. He's her brother, isn't he?"

Told, Dillon thought. For the second time he found himself glancing back at Rita, to see if she could offer any illumination to him.

"Now, Joe," Loretta repeated sharply. "Let him alone. I'm warning you, Joe. We've had quite enough of this for today; quite enough. It isn't the time or the place now. We're a little upset."

"But I tell you that he's got to know about it," Farrell said, with his usual habit of asserting manly and unquestioned authority in all family conferences. "It can't help, putting it off, Lorry. He's just got to go up there and talk to that Rutherfurd character tomorrow morning, man to man. Don't you start backing away from this thing, John. I'll go up there with you myself, if you want me to. What the hell do they think they're going to sweep under the rug, anyway? You know what I'd tell them, John? I'd tell them that I happened to be Chris Dillon's brother, that's all, and that if I had to tear their whole goddam hick town wide open to find what really happened to her—"

But it seemed to be a declaration in another language to Dillon. He had eaten very little since Saturday night; slept less. So he got up now, principally in order to get Joe Farrell's hands off his shoulders.

"Take it easy," he said. "We know what happened. She was walking home from the movies when that car hit her. Chief Rutherfurd explained the whole thing to me Saturday night. You got any more coffee out there, Rita?"

"Well, maybe not quite all," Farrell informed him. "It's beginning to look like the guy sold you a bill of goods, John. Because from what we just heard . . . the Riley kid here has a lot different story. Tell him, Peg."

'Oh, shut up!" Loretta commanded him, and in a hard, furious tone. "You'd do a lot, you would—if you could use your big flapping mouth to do it with. Listen, Johnny. There's no need to get yourself all upset again, but maybe Chris was out Saturday night with some fellow up there. They'd been slipping off two or three times a week with this Roy Vinson, whoever he is, and some friend of his, and Peg's aunt caught them sneaking in about three in the morning last Thursday. So perhaps we ought to . . . But drink your coffee first. We're only trying to decide what to do now. Do you understand what I'm talking about?"

He was not sure. Perhaps he did; perhaps he did not. He glanced at Peg Riley this time, and found her beginning to whimper miserably. Something wrong, he began to realize then; something about Chris. Before he could think of anything to say, however, Mrs. Riley, a stout, matronly woman of great firmness, shifted herself a little uncomfortably and began explaining to him.

"I'm afraid that we had no chance to tell you about this until now," she said. "Afraid and ashamed, Mr. Dillon, because that's the truth of it. But this damned little hellion of mine here only told the story to her father and me when we got home from the wake last night. And I'm very sorry to say that they were indeed slipping out at night up there, and that my sister Annie caught them doing it. She threatened to call you right away then, and to pack the two of them straight home, if they kept it up. Well, my sweet Peg never did do it again, or so she insists to me. But at the same time, without intending to hint anything at all about your poor Chris, I suppose you know how she was sometimes. She was the kind that liked a bit of innocent mischief for herself. She always did, Mr. Dillon. You must know that. And I've got to say it to you."

Yes, Dillon found himself thinking numbly, she always did. A firm hand had been almost the last thing Mamma had whispered to him; but what kind of a firm hand had Johnny Dillon kept? He had let a kid like that go up all alone to Hazard Lake, hadn't he? And if Rita was right, he had let her go up there because . . . A little of the coffee spilled out of the cup. Quickly and quietly Rita came over with a couple of paper napkins and mopped up.

"Let me get you a drink," she suggested. "I think you need it, Johnny. Wait a minute."

"All right," Dillon said. "Thanks, Rita." But his mental reactions were very slow. He did not want a drink. All he wanted was to understand what Mrs. Riley was saying to him. "But what's all this about Saturday night?" he asked Loretta. "What happened?"

"Well, it was Chris's night off," Loretta admitted reluctantly to him. "And it seems that she and Peg were going to go to the movies together, only at the last minute one of the other girls got sick, and Peg had to take over for her. But perhaps Chris didn't go to the movies at all. She told Peg's aunt that she was going to the second show at nine o'clock, but then she stopped at the drive-in a little before that, and called someone. It might have been this fellow Roy Vinson, Johnny. It might not. We don't know yet."

"Chris?" Dillon said. It was still incomprehensible to him. "But I told her," he added anxiously. "That's not true, Lorry. No dates at all, I said, unless Peg's aunt knew the fellow, and said that it was okay. And she wouldn't lie to me about anything like that. Not Chris."

"No," Loretta said, touching his hand quietly. "Of course. Not Chris. Or she wouldn't mean to, Johnny. But that's over the bridge now, what she meant. She'd promise anything at all she was asked to promise, and then the minute she was out by herself . . . Maybe she never met anyone at all Saturday night. Peg isn't sure. But of course if she did, if she called this Vinson fellow from the drive-in, and if he picked her up on the road later, so that Peg's aunt wouldn't know about it, then it certainly seems to me that he has a few questions to answer. One of us will just have to go up and talk about this to Chief Rutherfurd. I don't think it ought to be you, however. You've been under pretty much of a strain, Johnny. It might be better if—"

"And I tell you no," Joe Farrell again insisted to her. "He's the cop in the family, ain't he? Let him do it. They've got a nice little home town clique working together on this thing, Lorry, and if we just sit around on our duffs down here talking about it . . . It's up to John, I tell you."

"Open your mouth just once more," Loretta told him, in a quiet conversational manner, but with the impression of much savage force held in restraint, "and I'm going to smash you right in the face with this butter dish. You'd better believe me now—and you'd better let Johnny alone for a minute. He's not himself. Don't you pay any attention to that kind of talk, Johnny. It's all wind and hot air, the way it usually is. What he'd do! Chief Rutherfurd doesn't know a thing about this. Peg admits she was a lot too frightened to tell anybody until she told her mother last night. Would you mind repeating exactly what you said to us, Peg?"

"And speak up," Mrs. Riley directed ominously. "We'll listen to all that broken-hearted weeping and wailing later on, madam, when I warrant you there'll be damned good reason for it. Well?"

"But that's it," Peg Riley blubbered at him. "Honest, Johnny. Chris came to the drive-in that night about half past eight, and said maybe she'd get a date for herself instead of going to some silly old cowboy movie. Well, you'd better not, I told her, not with that Roy Vinson. Aunt Anna told you he was no good. Suppose she finds out? But I saw her make a call over at the pay phone, anyway, kind of tossing her head a little, and grinning at me, and then putting out her tongue at me. And that's all I know about it. I had to go out with an order, and when I came back she wasn't around any more. I don't know who she called, or where she went, either. I never saw her after that."

Once again Dillon could feel a sense of painful attention to the words uttered, without quite grasping them.

"But the chief told me," he insisted to Loretta. "She was walking home from the movies that night, and a car hit her. They found her like that. They found her lying beside one of the roads up there."

"And maybe that's what happened," Rita said to quiet him. "We're just not sure, Johnny. We'll have to find out. Suppose Loretta and I drove up there tomorrow morning?"

"Loretta and you?" Dillon said. He was still numbly bewildered, but it seemed to him that Joe Farrell had a lot more sense than that, anyway. "But I'm going myself," he insisted to her. "Don't argue, Rita. This whole thing is my responsibility and my fault. I let her go up there, didn't I?"

"Will you please stop talking about faults and responsibilities?" Loretta demanded, glaring around angrily at Joe Farrell. "I'm not going to let you go up there, Johnny; not by yourself. You don't know the condition you're in. Just look in the mirror."

"You're exhausted," Rita put in anxiously. "Please, Johnny. You've been walking around in a complete fog for three days."

"I'm going up there," Dillon told her, flattening out his voice carefully. "I'm going up there first thing tomorrow morning, Rita. Now that's finished."

But it was not quite finished. Loretta and Rita went

out to the kitchen, and began murmuring together. Presently they came back.

"Then all right," Loretta agreed. "If you want to, Johnny. If you go over to Rita's tonight instead of staying here all alone, and have a good dinner for yourself, and a night's sleep—and if you let her drive you up tomorrow. Will you do that much?"

So he said that he would; very minor conditions, Dillon thought them. Later on in the afternoon he let Rita drive him out to Rockaway Beach, talking quite normally to her, but with an idea that there was a strained inward anxiety gathering together in him. For a while he could not understand what the anxiety indicated, however; what caused it. Was it something about Chrissy—dead Chrissy? Was it the thought of a man he had never seen, and knew nothing about—this Roy Vinson? What?

But the anxiety would not clarify itself for Dillon. It only remained evident in him, as if there was something he had to do for Chrissy now; some necessary action to take; something that might help her a little, or help himself. But help in what way? He could not imagine that. After supper he accepted two sleeping pills from Rita, and Mrs. Nielsen prepared the guest bedroom. He went up early, about eight o'clock, took the sleeping pills, smoked one more cigarette and fell asleep almost immediately.

When he woke up about four in the morning the same idea of hot, tight anxiety, urging him on to some sort of obscure action, was still present. He sat over by the bedroom window until dawn, smoking more cigarettes, but still unable to rid himself of the anxiety, or to understand the meaning of it; nothing clear. At last he heard the Nielsens stirring around. He got up, went into the bathroom, checked his big service revolver carefully and put it back in his belt holster.

He did not understand why he did that, either. All he knew—or perhaps all that he permitted himself to know—was that some sort of decision lay just under the surface of full consciousness in him. And it was exactly the right place for it, Dillon felt. He did not want it out in the open yet, with a lot of moral questions to be settled, perhaps this, maybe that, but quiet and waiting until he put forth the deliberate effort of reaching down for it. Outwardly, however, he appeared altogether composed. He had breakfast downstairs, said goodbye to Mr. and Mrs. Nielsen, thanked them and at half past eight started out in her car with Rita for Hazard Lake.

It was a long drive, more than three hundred miles, and the sleeping pills still had him a bit groggy, slow in everything now, and detached from everything. So Rita drove the whole way, and when she spoke to him Dillon answered her. When she did not speak to him he looked out at the countryside, or dozed fitfully. Even in his waking moments his mind felt oddly dry and remote to him; the anxiety, and with it the idea of a now-decided but still unclear action to be taken, persisted mile after mile; and it was impossible to feel that he was an ordinary part of whatever happened to be going on at the moment. He had a slight headache, too, and of course the stomach bothered him. He was very thirsty. About noontime they stopped near Albany for a sandwich and a cup of coffee, and afterward in the men's washroom he again checked his service revolver. Primed and loaded, all right; everything set. He went back to the car.

From Albany they took the big new expressway north to Lake George, and about half past two, having dozed off again, he discovered that they were on a narrow, two-lane road leading them straight west into the central Adirondack preserve. It was pretty rugged country. Every so often now they passed through a small mountain village, or saw a stream rushing along the side of the road; and then there would be nothing but the Adirondack woods again, pine, oak, maple, white birch, narrow valleys, and sun-bathed slopes and peaks looming up higher and higher in the distance.

Beautiful country, Rita said. Yes, Dillon agreed, yes, it was, making very sure that he sounded like Johnny Dillon to her, the one she knew, and not the other part of him that appeared to be getting heavier and more solid in him with each minute. Rita knew him, and Rita must remember how he had felt that time about Eddie McManus, and about people not fit to walk the earth, even; so very careful with Rita. Very obediently, then, whenever Rita pointed them out, he admired cloud shadows drifting across wooded slopes, and every ten minutes or so, when the other presence in him wanted to feel very sure once more about the service revolver, he contrived to press it in against himself with his left elbow. It began to be a great comfort feeling it. Then the anxiety would ease off somewhat. But first, he warned himself, there would have to be a complete discussion about this thing with Chief Rutherfurd; no losing control yet. He had to know about it one way or the other. And then, when he did know . . . The steady tire chug began to impress a monotonous refrain into his head. If and when, the refrain went; if and when, Chrissy; if and when. Don't worry.

About four o'clock they drove through the big resort town of North Falls, and twenty minutes later began to pick up the first Hazard Lake signs. It was even necessary for them to pass Jack Riley's King of the North Snack Bar on the way in—a round, modernistic building, all glass and chromium, with an open service counter in front and a glittering soda fountain behind that.

There was, Dillon observed, business as usual at this

hour. It might be that the season had opened and closed a bit early up here for poor little Chris, but there was still a heavy smell of hamburgers and fried onions as they went by, a bit sickening to him; he could see the car hops scurrying from counter to customer in short skirts, trim little white aprons and saucily tilted Dutch caps; and so he made a rather foolish mistake at that point. He twisted himself around beside Rita, to look back at them, and caught her watching him. "What's the matter?" he said. "What's the look for?"

"Nothing," Rita said. "Nothing, Johnny. Just a look, that's all."

Now they could see the village ahead of them. It lay clustered around the far end of the lake, with the business part at the tip of it, and the residential area straggling out on both sides. The most prominent feature was a three-story red-brick building with an open tower in the center, and a big clock facing them; obviously the Town Hall.

On their side of the water was a section of auto courts, hamburger stands and gas stations; on the other, what appeared to be the class residential neighborhood. Over there Dillon could see big comfortable white houses, a private dock or two and wide sunny lawns. A motor boat flashed ahead on blue water, and a couple of small sails drifted lazily. ". . . went swimming this morning," Dillon remembered. "Me and Peg. Gosh, I miss you, Johnny. I must be crazy."

It was a very good memory for him. It made him feel quietly controlled in mind and body, very cunning with Rita and extremely alert without appearing to be. There was a five-story hotel on Main Street, old-fashioned but comfortable, and as soon as he was alone in his room he washed up and put on a clean shirt. But even then his eyes looked just a little peculiar to him in

34

the bathroom mirror—dry, dull, a bit more starey than he wanted them. The sleeping pills?

He'd have to watch himself, all right. Rita knew every flicker of expression in Johnny Dillon. And what had she and Loretta been whispering about in the kitchen yesterday? What had they cooked up between them—that Rita mustn't let him slip away by himself for two minutes? He washed his eyes out a second time, attempting to rub some life into them, put on his tie and his coat, and then consulted the small telephone book, Hazard Lake and vicinity, on the bedside table. There was only one Vinson listed there, a Mrs. Roy J., Sr., probably the mother. The address for her was 147 Lake Avenue.

He could have written the address down. He did not bother—147 Lake Avenue. He'd remember it, Dillon thought. After that he went down to the lobby, found Rita waiting for him and walked out with her to the usual small town Main Street.

They found the Hazard Lake Police Department around on one side of the Town Hall, off an alley that ran between that building and an adjoining hardware store. A police cruiser waited outside, no one in it, and in the office there was a desk, a telephone, a wooden railing that divided the room into halves and a couple of long benches.

But it was not the kind of police department that Detective Dillon would have recognized at first glance. The office was deserted, too, and when the phone rang and rang there was nobody to answer it. But presently a tall, gaunt man of about sixty came in from another part of the building, dressed in a wrinkled uniform and wearing a gold braided chief's cap. Then Dillon got up, introduced himself and Rita, and shook hands.

Rutherfurd answered the phone, keeping his voice

lowered. He was a gloomy-looking man with a top-heavy mountaineer slouch, deep hollows in each cheek and a bonily ridged, rather ugly forehead. He kept his eyes down around Dillon's necktie during his telephone conversation. Then he opened a gate in the rail and ushered them on into a smaller and more private office.

In there a barred door on the left led off to a few empty lockup cells, and a dusty window at the rear permitted a view out over the back yard. They all sat down, Rutherfurd behind the desk, Dillon and Rita in front of it. The facts about Peg Riley were explained to Rutherfurd then. He listened, head down, gloomy dark eyes shifting about. Once or twice he interjected a brief, sensible question; at other times he pushed the gold braided cap around on his desk in what appeared to be a dourly abstracted manner.

And then it was his turn, Dillon waiting for him to explain now, and waiting patiently and courteously. But Rutherfurd did not appear to relish that it was his turn. He had the manner, Dillon granted to him, of someone not too happy about himself, or about what he would have to admit at this moment. Still dour, he stroked one side of his long, prominent jaw, then the other. Well, he began after that, he had no idea how familiar Mr. Dillon might be with the ordinary course of an official police investigation into something of this nature. So perhaps the first thing to explain . . .

One picture, it came to Dillon; a thousand words. He got out his wallet, flipped it open silently and displayed the department shield to Chief Rutherfurd.

"Oh," Rutherfurd said, inspecting it over a pair of rimless eyeglasses. "Yes. I see. One of us. I only wish I knew whether that's going to make it a bit easier for me, Dillon, or a lot worse. I'm not very proud of myself.

But to begin with, she was found a mile or two out on the North Falls Road, near a picnic grounds that we call Mountainview Park. A cab driver from town spotted her out there, or the yellow raincoat she had on. That's the first we knew about it. I believe the call came in here about twenty minutes past eleven Saturday night."

Dillon put the wallet back in his pocket, still silently; but he could remember the raincoat. He had bought it for Chris this past spring, after the most explicit instructions as to cut and color, and so he found himself glancing about vaguely, not to keep thinking of such matters. The one window in here must be pretty dirty, he told himself. Outside it was still a sunny and pleasant July afternoon, but in here everything seemed to have taken on an odd, reddish look—the desk, Rutherfurd's gaunt, gloomy face, the worn matting on the floor, the distempered brown walls. He could hear voices and footsteps in the upstairs hall, and a phone ringing in one of the other offices.

"Could she say anything?" Rita asked quietly. "Was she still conscious, chief?"

The big knuckled mountaineer hands spread apart reluctantly, indicating no. But of course stolidity was the only possible manner for Chief Rutherfurd here; it was again the precise way that Detective Dillon would have behaved in similar circumstances. Multiple head and neck injuries, Rutherfurd told them; exactly the same effect on Miss Dillon as if a car had struck her at high speed, knocked her aside into a stone wall near the road and kept going. So at the time it had looked plain enough to him—hit and run.

"At the time?" Dillon repeated. His head ached badly. Something appeared to be getting tighter and tighter around it; clamping in. "Maybe I'm a little

37

slow," he said. "I'm sorry. But what does that mean—'at the time'? You trying to tell me something, Rutherfurd?"

The gaunt man got up from behind his desk, walked over to the door to the other office and closed it. He also closed the lockup door. Then he came back beside Dillon's chair, standing just a little behind it, with his hands in his back pockets and his big shoulders hunched.

"Or tell myself," he announced finally. At least he had the manner of a slow, careful man, Dillon realized; but a capable professional one? That had to be proved now. "But I'd like you to remember that Mountainview Park is on the way out to Jack Riley's house, where I understand Miss Dillon was living up here, and I had to assume that she was on her way home from the movie show when the thing happened to her. That's where Mrs. Riley had told me she'd been. And the movie let out at five minutes of eleven, remember; she had to walk all the way back to Jack Riley's house, with no car; and so in fifteen or twenty minutes she would have got out about as far as where the cab driver found her. So it all seemed plain enough to me. But again at the time, Dillon."

"Okay," Dillon said. He even managed a tight grin over at Rita, to show her that there was absolutely no sweat about this; that all he wanted from Rutherfurd was the straight story. "I know how it goes, Rutherfurd. You look around at what happened, dig up all the material evidence that you can and then figure it out. So what material evidence did you dig up?"

If any at all, he thought. Getting redder and redder in here.

"Well, the nature of her injuries," Rutherfurd said, but again reluctantly. "The position of her head against that stone wall; the fact that her purse and her right shoe were still out in the road. But I'll have to explain to you about Mountainview Park. It's on the other side of the highway out there, Dillon, and it has a lookout built up facing the lake with a stone wall around front. I imagine that wall is about seventy or eighty feet up over the highway. You get a pretty view from there on a clear day, or a clear night, for that matter. A lot of our young people slip up there after dark; but nothing like this ever happened before that I remember. If it had—"

"Always a first time," Dillon said. "I wouldn't let it worry me, Rutherfurd. Then what else did you go ahead and assume?"

"Now, please," Rita begged him. "The chief is only trying to explain to you how—"

"Okay, okay," Dillon said. He took her hand, even; very cunning. There was still nothing for him to get excited about. He remembered that address, didn't he? Of course—147 Lake Avenue. He remembered, all right.

"You mean," he told Rutherfurd, "that she wasn't hit by a car at all. You mean she was knocked over that wall from Mountainview Park. But when did you begin thinking about that, Rutherfurd? What gave you the idea finally?"

"Fellow in town," Rutherfurd said. But had he glanced covertly at Rita before saying it, and Rita at him? Dillon flicked his eyes at each of them, a quick, hot glance, but caught nothing. "Fellow named Willie Neale. I don't suppose there's any real harm in the boy; a natural, you'd call him. But once in a while he hangs around Mountainview Park at night, trying to see whatever he can in one of the cars. And now his story, but only so far as we can credit, remember, is that he saw a good deal up there last Saturday night.

"The unfortunate thing is that he never told me until a couple of hours ago. He isn't too strong in the head, you understand. So I got hold of it first through some-body else, and then talked to Willie about it. And his story . . . you're sure, are you, that you want the whole thing straight out, Dillon? It's not pretty."

"I believe yes," Dillon said. But why had he snapped off that yes for Rutherfurd like the crack of a whip? What was the matter with him? Rita would notice. "Just tell me the way it comes, Rutherfurd. What did he see up there?"

It developed then that he had seen a gray Cadillac. Saturday night it had been the only car in Mountain-view Park, according to Willie; but then, Rutherfurd said, it had been drizzling off and on since early in the afternoon. He had slipped up through the woods to-ward it, in any event, and was soon close enough to hear a girl crying, and a man talking to her.

The man had sounded very angry to Willie. He had been saying something about what did she think he was, anyway, a high school boy? She had chased after him for two weeks; she had called him tonight; and she had come up here with him. How old was she, anyway? Then the girl managed to jump out, still crying, with her yellow raincoat torn where the fellow tried to grab her, and of course as soon as she opened the car door the inside light had snapped on. The girl Willie Neale had never seen before. The fellow he had. The fellow was Roy Vinson.

"And he's positive?" Dillon said. He wanted to be very sure about that, the one last thing. Now there was an extraordinary calmness in him, everything settled in regard to 147 Lake Avenue, but the damned red sun-light kept bothering him, and he decided to squint against it, still keeping his head carefully lowered from Rita. "What did you think about that kind of a story, Rutherfurd? You're the head of the department up here, or you got the uniform on. Did you believe it or not?"

"Hard to say," Rutherfurd announced stolidly. "With Willie. But after that he says they got around on the other side of the car from him, where he could hear the two of them, but not see them. Then the girl cried out something that contradicts the whole thing, as I see it. 'No,' she says. 'Leave me alone! Johnny, Johnny!' But why would she say anything like that, if it was Vinson with her? You see what I mean, don't you? Who's Johnny?"

Rita whispered one or two very soft words to herself, and turned her head. Dillon only put his hands between his knees and rubbed them in a neat, brisk manner . . . 147 Lake Avenue.

"Well, that was me," he told Rutherfurd. "That fits, all right. I'm Johnny."

"Oh," Rutherfurd said. "Of course. Well . . . you're sure you want me to go on with this, Johnny?"

"I don't think so," Rita said. "Not any more. Please, Johnny."

"Let him tell it," Dillon warned her quietly. "The whole thing. I want him to. Go on, Rutherfurd."

There was very little more, however. The fellow argued with her, and she started to run. Willie couldn't see where she ran, but it was over in the direction of the stone wall. After that, with the fellow yelling at her from back at the car, perhaps warning her, Willie had heard a quick, scraping rush, and another scream; then nothing.

"The fellow," Dillon said, parting his hands now, and staring down fixedly at his left palm, and then at his right one. "The fellow, the fellow, the fellow. Why do you keep on putting it like that, Rutherfurd? You know who it was. You had to wait, of course, for somebody like this Willie Neale to tell you. But now you know, don't you?"

"As you like," Rutherfurd conceded heavily. "But you'd have to know Willie Neale to appreciate what kind of a witness he'll make. I think we'll both have to take it a bit slow and easy yet, Johnny. But if his story holds up—"

"Well, naturally," Dillon said. "You hear, Rita? If the story holds up. I told him about Peg Riley before I heard even a damned word about this. I gave him the guy's name. But there's still a big question about it. He's just not sure, Rita."

"Johnny," Rutherfurd put in, after another brief pause, "I know how you feel about this. I don't blame you. And I don't blame you because I know exactly how I've handled the whole thing so far. But I've already called in the state police on this thing, and in an hour or so they're going to have a couple of technicians in Mountainview Park checking the whole area for tire marks and whatever else they can find. I'm going to do everything that I can about this. I was out there myself just before you got here, and I noticed a jut of rock on the way down. Now if she hit against that, and I think she must have, it would have flung her over to the other side of the road, exactly where she was found afterward. You've got to remember that the impact marks, whether a car hit her at high speed, or whether she fell seventy or eighty feet from the dropoff, would be pretty much the same. I told you that we found her on the other side of the highway, and with her head all twisted against a stone wall. What would you have believed yourself in those circumstances?"

"Okay, okay," Dillon repeated. He had begun rubbing the hands once more. "That isn't the point here. The point is how you're going to handle it from now on, Rutherfurd—and I'd certainly like to know about that,

42

too. Have you talked to this Vinson yet? Have you got his story?"

Rutherfurd gave them a grim nod.

"He'll be in," he said. "I wouldn't worry about that, Johnny. And say anything you want to me. I don't think you can add a hell of a lot to what I've said to myself by this time. But losing our heads about it isn't going to help anyone at all, remember. Now I've already made a seven o'clock appointment for tonight with our prosecutor up here, Charley Robinson, to discuss the matter. Would you like to sit down with us, and get his opinion?"

"I don't know," Dillon said. He had not been following too closely. Johnny, Johnny . . . He had to think back a little. "But suppose you give me a ring later on at the hotel," he said. "I've got a damned rotten headache, and I'd better do something about it. But if Chris called him about half past eight, Rutherfurd, which Peg Riley told me she did, and if Willie Neale saw them up in Mountainview Park at eleven, then they must have been somewhere else for a couple of hours. Try that angle, can't you? Who saw them together? Where did they go? What did they do? Don't just sit around in this office until people come in and tell you the things you ought to be finding out for yourself. You've got a job to do up here. Then get out and do it. What the hell kind of a police chief are you, anyway?"

Rita got up anxiously.

"It's only three hours ago," she said. "The chief is doing everything that he can, now that he knows about it. Please, Johnny."

"I thought it was four full days," Dillon said. "Sorry. My mistake, Rutherfurd. But you don't understand about these things, Rita. They won't find a damned thing up there now in Mountainview Park. It's too late. You've got to catch something like this in the first couple of hours, or it blows wide open on you. How many other cars do you think have been up there in Mountainview Park by this time? How many other tire marks? They should have been over the ground right away, the second it happened, and this fellow knows it. I tell you it's too late now!"

"Say anything you like," Rutherfurd growled at him, or perhaps at himself. "Better out than in, Johnny. I won't complain about it. We have to do what we can now, and that's all."

"Come back to the hotel," Rita said. "You don't look right, Johnny. Lie down for a couple of hours. Try to rest. And then I think . . . please, Johnny."

"Please, nothing," he said. It was difficult for him to keep still now, and so he moved over a little toward the back window, stuck his hands into his coat pockets and then took them out almost immediately. "How has this whole thing been handled? And you expect me to sit here and not even open my mouth about it? Joe Farrell was right, maybe. They're trying to sweep it under the rug, Rita."

"I don't think you believe that," Rutherfurd said quietly. "I hope not. But if you want my own personal opinion, Johnny, I think Willie Neale saw exactly what he told me he saw, and with one or two other facts to back him up I also think that we'll have a damned good chance of proving it in court against Roy Vinson. But as I said before, it's not going to do any good losing our heads about it. We'll be fighting money, for one thing. Old Vinson ran the bank up here until he died two years ago, and he seemed to be a decent enough man.

"The son, I'm afraid, is another proposition entirely. Twenty-two or three; into a couple of Ivy League colleges after prep school, and then out of them in short order; and the kind of a mother that spoils him rotten. There was something like this—not quite so bad, however—with a girl over in North Falls some months ago, but the mother squashed it. I suppose there was a little money involved. But she won't squash this, Johnny, and I give you my word she won't."

It was just firm and quiet enough to be convincing to Dillon. He faced around from the window, a little ashamed of himself.

"Think I'll take it," he announced huskily. "Sorry, Rutherfurd. You figure you can put it all together, then?"

"I don't see why not," Rutherfurd said. "He's the kind of a fellow that hangs around the hotel bar here in town, but he wasn't there Saturday night. I've already checked. What he did, I suppose, was to pick up your sister on the road somewhere, since you tell me that Jack Riley's wife, knowing the kind he is, didn't want her to go out with him again. Then they probably drove over to North Falls for a drink and a dance in one of the night spots.

"Now if they did that, we're going to have somebody else to place them together; a waiter, or maybe a bartender. But first, Johnny, I'd like to get a sworn statement from him, because he's the kind that's going to deny ever seeing her that night. I know he is. He'd face you down about the sun rising in the east every morning, if there was any advantage for Mr. Roy Vinson in doing it.

"But that's fine, I'd say. Let him deny it. We'll catch him out in his first lie with Willie Neale, and anybody else we can get hold of, and he'll start gilding the lily, which will only get him in deeper and deeper, Johnny. You know how that goes. You must have seen it yourself often. The more lies they start to tell, the more mistakes they make, and the sooner they hang themselves. So I wish you'd do what Miss Nielsen wants you to do. Go back to the hotel, lie down there for a couple of hours, and then, if you'd like, talk to me and Charley Robinson tonight about this with a clear head. What's your room number?"

And all at once it seemed to be about the best thing to do all around to Detective Dillon; in fact, the only thing. What kind of crazy idea had been in his head about going out to 147 Lake Avenue, and attending to this Roy Vinson personally? What good would that do? Detective Dillon wasn't a mad dog. He had four or five commendations from the department already, and a gold medal. This would have to be done in the right way. Chrissy was dead. Nothing could change that part, whatever he did. He had to face up to cold fact here.

"All right," he admitted finally. "Maybe I am a little bushed out, chief. I don't seem to be thinking too well. But I've had this damned headache bothering me all afternoon. Do you have any aspirins, Rita?"

"We'll get some," she said. "There's a drugstore just outside the hotel, Johnny. We'll stop there."

So he shook hands with Chief Rutherfurd very calmly and quietly, and got his hat. He felt more like himself, at long last; even the sunlight had become normal for him, a bright, warm yellow, not that disturbingly ominous red any more. Rutherfurd said something else, and Rita answered him. Then the desk phone rang, and at almost the same instant the door to the outer office was thrown open. A stout, red-faced town patrolman put his head in at them.

"Got Roy Vinson out here," he announced to Rutherfurd. "He was over to Placid all afternoon, chief. You ready for him now?"

So in the end it was not cold and deliberate at all for Chris Dillon's brother. A thing happened to him. All at once he saw the patrolman's face blood-red before him in the office doorway; he saw everything blood-red; and there was just one sharp, perfectly audible snap in his ears. The tightness around them burst wide open.

He began to move. He got around Rita calmly enough, but a bit hurriedly, because he understood that everything would have to be done with the utmost rapidity from now on, and before they were ready for him. He got past the desk, too, and past Rutherfurd. The stout patrolman blinked at him, grinned a little uncertainly and backed off.

"What?" Rutherfurd said. But the telephone call had distracted him for the moment; he did nothing but turn his head clumsily. "What was that, Jerry?"

By then, however, there was only the patrolman to handle, and of course Rita. She was a lot quicker than Rutherfurd, but the chances were that she had caught Dillon's expression a moment ago. She knew at once. She came after him.

"No," she said. "Johnny. Johnny! Oh, my God. Stop him! He's got his service revolver! Chief!"

Yes, Dillon was telling himself. Two or three bare seconds; no more. So he plunged ahead into that darkly glittering column of July sunlight, got the patrolman with his left hand and flung him aside.

It was Rita who spoiled everything. She hit him from the back, straight-arming him over to one side of the door, and by the time he had recovered himself both Rutherfurd and the town patrolman were at him. Rutherfurd was a big, powerful man, too, and Dillon could fight him only with the one hand. He already had his service revolver in the other one. So they crashed back into the office wall, all three of them, and they got Dillon to his knees.

It was another matter keeping him there. Twice he managed to push up against them, even with all that dead weight on his shoulders, but the third time they held him spread-eagled against the wall, and Rutherfurd twisted the service revolver out of his hand. It was all quite silent now; not a word uttered. Rita, deathly pale, had enough sense to run over and close the office door while they were still wrestling around madly. Then she began talking to Dillon, standing with her back against the door, and trying to sound very quiet and sensible for him.

Rutherfurd talked, too. They could have been talking in a pure vacuum, however. He felt sweat dripping down his face, and he could hear himself breathing in hoarse, anguished gasps. He could hear nothing else. But he did not seem to be struggling any more; no reason for it. They had the gun. So he let Rutherfurd sit him down in a chair, finally, and keep him there. The office door was still closed. Rita, shaking visibly, was still standing against it.

"Now do just what I tell you," Rutherfurd ordered the cop Jerry. "This thing never happened in here today, Jerry, and remember it didn't. I don't know what I was thinking about. I never should have told him the whole story. It's my fault. Get Vinson to hell home out of here, and keep your mouth shut. Now mind what I say, Jerry. Nothing like this ever happened. Do you want a drink, Johnny?"

He provided one. Dillon got it down one way or another. Then they made him stay in the office for some time, until long after the police cruiser had driven off. Rita straightened his tie, brushed off his coat and picked up his hat. They did not, however, give him back his service revolver. At ten minutes past five they walked back to the hotel with him, Rita on one side, Frank Rutherfurd on the other.

They even went up to his room with him, undressed him to pants and socks and made him lie down. He was listless by now. He didn't care what they did with him. He just lay there. Soon there was another man, who snapped open a doctor's bag, stuck a needle in Dillon's shoulder and talked quietly and soothingly to him.

But he did not pay much attention to the doctor, either. There was another thought in his head, and it seemed to him a good, sound and consoling thought. All right, it told him. He had missed the first time because he had been careless and stupid about the whole thing. But the second time . . .

He opened his eyes later, with much effort, and saw Rita murmuring over in one corner of the room, and Frank Rutherford murmuring back soberly to her. After that he drifted off little by little, not caring again, and slept straight through, for something like nineteen and a half hours, until one o'clock Thursday afternoon.

CHAPTER 3

A bit later on that day, when he and Rita were driving home in the car, they had the chance for a long, quiet talk together. It must have been all the strain on him, Rita thought. Burying Chris first; then Peg Riley's story, still not sure of anything; then Rutherfurd's story, and sure of everything; and all at once, right there in the next room to him . . .

"But don't you ever scare me like that again," she said, giving him a surprisingly helpless and appealing look for Rita. "If you could only have seen yourself, Johnny. You were fighting against them like a wild animal."

"Guess I was," he admitted miserably. The night's sleep had helped; Rita was helping more; but even so he did not care to think back now over that scene in

Rutherfurd's office. "All I know is that something snapped in me, hon. If I ever got out through that door, I would have emptied the revolver into him. I know it. And if you want to hear something else, I think I was planning it all the way up yesterday. Maybe I was lucky it happened like that. The other way I might have done it to him in cold blood, Rita."

"I wouldn't quite say in cold blood," she told him, and then shivered delicately. "You haven't been acting right since Saturday night, Johnny; since it happened. That's what had me and Loretta so worried about this. I believe you were in what they call shock, actually."

"I suppose," Dillon said, managing to grin feebly. "I can tell you that it was one hell of a feeling, anyway. All I could remember was that it had to be my fault; that I was the one who let her go up there when you and Loretta said I was crazy. But I never thought I could lose control of myself like that. I felt like a blind man stumbling around on an empty lot. No more landmarks."

"But why should you blame yourself?" Rita demanded. "You weren't responsible. The thing happened, that's all, and it happened because poor little Chris didn't pay any attention to what you told her. She always tried to act grown up and sophisticated with people, and he got the wrong idea about her, and began making cracks, and she just never understood what he was suggesting to her. She was too much of a kid, Johnny."

"I don't know about that," he persisted doggedly. "But what I do know is that I had the same kind of an idea once before, hon; I mean about putting a lot of bullets into someone just as fast as I could pull the trigger on him. You remember when Eddie McManus got shot dead this April? It was the same thing with me; exactly the same. I didn't want to arrest those fellows, Rita. I wanted to kill them. So what kind of a human being am I, anyway? Maybe not much of a one, eh?"

"I'll worry about that," Rita said, reaching over firmly to twine fingers with him. "I'll take a chance, Johnny. You stand for the right things, remember. You want a clean, decent world fit for people to live in, and you try to do something about it. But the dirty half of the coin you can't stick. That's your trouble. You despise and I suppose even hate it too much."

"Made a clean, decent world for you," he mumbled. "Look at the way I've been acting about us all along, Rita. I took advantage of you. I know it. It wasn't right."

"Oh, for heaven's sake," Rita said, getting a fine color in her. "John Patrick Dillon! Oh, you are a fool. Took advantage of me! All right, then; let me tell you something. I managed that whole Catskill weekend for us from start to finish. But I had the classical excuse, of course. I loved you very much, Johnny. I thought you needed me."

"And always will," Dillon promised, tightening his fingers on her. "Don't you ever go back on me, Rita. I could take a lot of things without hollering about them, but not that. What do you mean about arranging the whole weekend, though? I thought you just got your dates mixed up."

"Well, I did," Rita admitted. "But accidentally on purpose, Johnny. I put on a pretty good act, don't I? Now don't think I'm blaming your sisters for anything, but you certainly had to give up a lot for them, Johnny, and I think you gave up so much that you got yourself in the habit of it. Look at our relationship. Oh, you loved me, all right, I knew that, but on very definite terms. We had to wait until Chrissy was out of high school, anyway, and I just better resign myself or else. You made it rather painfully evident, I'd say. And then what happened?

"Then Eddie McManus got killed, and by that time you were so used to accepting responsibility for other people that you had to accept it for Eddie, too. You kept blaming yourself for that, and I could see it in you, just the way you're blaming yourself for Chris now. Pretty soon you weren't the same Johnny Dillon any more. I could feel something—well, hateful and violent in you. I suppose all of us have a dark brother to worry about, as I read once in a psychology book, but you let it get completely out of hand when that happened to Eddie. I knew what you intended to do to those two men, if you ever caught them. You had me frightened."

And the dark brother was not at all a bad term for what he had felt yesterday in Chief Rutherfurd's office, Dillon told himself. It fitted pretty good. He lit a cigarette for Rita, and passed it over.

"I suppose you're right," he admitted. "But people like that have to be paid out for what they do. You can't let them get away with it. If you did, then what kind of a world would we have?"

"But they get away with it every day," she pointed out. "And you don't let things like that happen, Johnny. They just do happen. You're not omniscient, are you? I knew, anyway, that you intended to pay them out; that they killed Eddie, and that what you were after was to kill them. Well, I didn't want anything like that to happen to you, or to us, I suppose. I wanted to get that crazy violence out of you.

"So I made up my mind, too. I wanted to show you what we really meant to one another; what we could make for ourselves, with any kind of a fair chance. It seemed to me that you would be one kind of man, if I ever succeeded in getting through to you, and another and much different kind if I didn't. And we were two people very much in love, weren't we? So you did need me, I decided, even if you wouldn't admit it to yourself; and you certainly needed a little help with that dark brother of yours. Well, I tried to give it to you the only way that I could think of. Smart girl. Because it didn't work out at all like that, did it?"

"It's going to," Dillon promised her. "From now on, Rita. You wait and see."

So it turned out to be a pretty good day for the two of them, after a very bad one. They got everything settled. In January, they decided, after Chrissy had been dead for six months, they would have a quiet wedding out in Rockaway Beach, and that seemed a very suitable decision to Dillon. Chrissy was gone now, after all, and nothing he could ever do to anyone was going to change that part. Rita knew what she was talking about. The business of the living was with the living. He would have to accept it about Chris.

And he certainly tried hard. He became accustomed to a lot of things that fall—to living all alone in the apartment; to making a fresh, clean start between him and Rita, the way it should have been the whole time; and most of all, whenever he thought of somebody named Roy Vinson, to immediately force the name out of his head. The thing that had almost happened in Rutherfurd's office must never be given even the least chance to happen again. Now he knew what he had gone up there to do. Why else had he looked in his room telephone book, and first thing? But Rutherfurd knew the town and the people, and the sensible thing was to let Rutherfurd handle it.

So by November the dark brother had become no more than an occasional and uncomfortable memory to him. No one else knew what he had tried to do but him and Rita, Rutherfurd and the patrolman; even Loretta was never told. Joe Farrell, of course, was a little disappointed in him. He just couldn't understand it, Joe said. Sitting around in New York, doing nothing at all, and letting that home town clique up there . . . "You don't have to understand it," Dillon told him. "And you don't have to keep talking about it, either. I'm letting Frank Rutherfurd handle the whole thing. Shut up, will you?"

But once or twice, naturally, he called Rutherfurd on the phone, or Rutherfurd called him, and everything seemed to be progressing in good order. They had located a waiter over in a North Falls roadhouse called The Pines, Dillon was informed, and he had identified two people whom he had served on the night of July 14th as Roy Vinson and Chris. So after that the first big jump had been negotiated. There was another witness now in addition to Willie Neale. The indictment had been handed in; Roy Vinson had been freed on high bail; and the trial, Rutherfurd thought, on charges of assault and attempted rape, perhaps even manslaughter, although the prosecutor was still a little dubious about that, was scheduled to come up sometime in January.

Yet that part struck Dillon as a first troubling coincidence—the trial in January, the wedding in January. But he had promised Rita, he remembered; no more dark brother. So in December they selected a new apartment on the Grand Concourse for themselves, and bought furniture. Four or five times a week he went out to Rockaway Beach to see her, achingly in love with her, even at the touch of a finger between them; and one Saturday night he brought her back to the apartment with him.

It was a mistake. He felt afterward that it had shown a contemptible weakness in Johnny Dillon. He had promised in Chris's memory a fresh start for them, but how had he kept his promise? Exactly the way he had kept another one to Mamma. And the idea troubled him more and more from then on, as if he had betrayed Chris a second time, with deliberate callousness. One night not long afterward he woke up suddenly, as if he had heard someone calling out to him from a vast distance. The voice he could not recognize. The two words he could.

Johnny, Johnny . . .

He had never enjoyed a really good appetite. Often at home he just opened up a can of tuna fish, or some baked beans. But now it worsened. He lost weight, with very little to spare; he became curt, touchy and withdrawn with other people, even with Rita; and one night in Loretta's house he snapped back venomously when Rita wanted to give him another helping of roast beef. He was at once repentant about that; but still, knowing that he had been entirely in the wrong, he found himself unable to respond to her afterward with tenderness and affection—almost with sudden hatred, rather. Then Loretta, always very quick to those moods of his, flashed back at him. She had always liked Rita.

"Now you just better watch out how you're acting," she commanded. "Don't you ever dare speak to Rita like that again; not in my house. What's the matter with you?"

"Nothing," he said, giving her back a low, ugly look over the table. "Not a damn thing. Just leave me alone, the whole bunch of you. You're always after me, one after another; Johnny, Johnny, Johnny. I might be getting a little tired of it, that's all."

Because it seemed to him now that they always were nagging lately, telling him to do this, or to do that; running his life. Whereas the thing he should have done up there in Hazard Lake months and months ago for poor little Chris, if he had been any kind of a man, and if he had only listened to what he himself wanted . . .

He suspected that it was the dark brother again, and this time with a cunning change of tactics against him. Unable to work on him through himself, it now apparently was attempting to work on him through Chris. But he could handle the dark brother all right, in his own manner. He didn't need any help for that, not even from Rita. He had sweated out a lot of things in his time; this, too. If only everybody would leave him alone! But no. His whole life had to be regulated for him—and little Chris rotting away month after month in Gate of Heaven, through his fault. Who cared about her any more? Who remembered her? But if her brother Johnny had no ties to anyone, and not to Rita, principally, he would have known what to do for her—and might yet. It would certainly be easy enough. Dillon the sharpshooter, if things didn't work out up there in Rutherfurd's way, wouldn't have to waste even five minutes thinking about it.

It came to the Christmas season. Bells tinkled when he came home from the precinct every night, but not to poor little Chris this year; there were colorful store windows all around, and holiday cheerfulness. It was not much of a holiday for Dillon, however, even though he made what effort he could for Rita's sake; and it turned out to be a worse New Year's. He called up Rutherfurd toward the end of the week, not having heard anything in some time, and discovered that the waiter had vanished.

"Just walked out on his job two days ago," Rutherfurd had to admit glumly. "I wouldn't worry about it yet, however. We'll locate him, all right. He's probably off on a drunk somewhere. We don't know, Johnny."

But it seemed to Dillon that he knew. Fritz the waiter could have been slipped enough money under the counter to go back to Germany or Austria, wherever he came from, because if he remembered Roy Vinson from last July, in time Roy Vinson would have remembered him, also. Now perhaps the witnesses were being tampered with up there. And what did Dillon intend to do about that part? He had done nothing at all so far. Joe Farrell was right. He was doing nothing at all now.

Johnny, Johnny . . .

New Year's Day there was a big family gathering out at Meg's house. And he had to attend, naturally; no choice in the matter. No choice in anything at all these days, not for him. Buy the furniture; find an apartment; enjoy a nice, happy life for himself; and forget Chris. Everyone agreed on that schedule for him, and without bothering to ask themselves if that was the schedule he himself wanted. Was it?

Johnny, Johnny . . .

He did not tell anyone about Fritz out at Meg's, but he ate poorly, even though forcing himself, drank a little, which was very unusual for him, and sat in the parlor afterward with the three brothers-in-law, while Rita and the girls were cleaning up out in the kitchen.

But how very simple it would all be, he began telling himself, if only he had complete freedom from Rita, and no obligations to her. Then Dillon the sharpshooter could drive up there to Hazard Lake and settle the thing as it should be settled. Assault and attempted rape; say eighteen months or two years, if Roy Vinson was ever convicted on those charges. And little Chris . . .

"How's the case going?" Joe Farrell wanted to know then. "You hear anything at all from that Toonerville cop, John?"

"Not a word," Dillon lied to him. But why? What was he afraid to admit now even to someone like Joe Farrell? "It's coming up sometime around the twentieth, Rutherfurd thinks. But I don't want to start talking about it, Joe. Not today."

"Okay, okay," Farrell said. He lit another cigar with that irritating salesman's complacency of his, and then shook his head regretfully. "But mark my words, John. You're not handling this in the right way. They're getting ready to pull something up there. I know they are. They're stalling around too much."

"So you know," Dillon said, a slight headache bothering him. He seemed to be getting them more and more lately. "Fine. You know a hell of a lot, don't you?"

"Well, he could have a point," Loretta's husband remarked thoughtfully. "It was a hell of a thing to happen to a kid like that. I caught Lorry crying out in the kitchen today. 'I still can't believe it,' she told me. 'I keep thinking about last New Year's.' That's when you had Chrissy and Rita out to our house, remember? You should have gone back up there once or twice, Johnny, to keep pushing the thing. We all ought to be doing a little something about it."

Gone back up there, Dillon thought. Were they crazy? If they only knew what had almost happened the first time . . .

"Then something like what?" he demanded, with an idea that the room walls were beginning to close in around him. "Talk sense, will you? Like sitting here over a lot of free booze, and shooting your mouths off about how all of you would have handled the thing? Now I don't want to talk about it, I tell you. Stop working on me."

He probably raised his voice on that last sentence. Rita heard him. She came out of the kitchen quickly.

"There's a little more coffee," she said. "Would you like some, Johnny?"

"But you didn't get yourself respected up there," Farrell pointed out. "You never went back after that first time, John. Now they figure they can push you around, and let the whole thing die a natural death. I don't know what's wrong with you lately. If it was my sister, I know what I'd have done about it. I'd have made it my business to talk to the guy himself, that's what. 'You remember Chris Dillon?' I'd have asked him. 'Well, I'm her brother, pal, and it's going to be you and me this time. A little different, hah?' Then I'd have taken him out into the woods up there, and by the time I got finished doing a job on that dirty—"

"Joe," Rita said. "Meg wants you to go upstairs and see how the baby is. She told me."

"You let him talk," Dillon ordered her. He discovered that he had got up abruptly. "He can always tell somebody else what to do, Rita. You know the kind, don't you?"

"Pretty tough around here," Farrell said, inspecting the end of his cigar casually. "Sure. But let me tell you this much, mister. I don't try to pass myself off as one of the toughest cops in the department, but I'm the kind that would have taken care of that fellow six months ago, if I had to steal a gun somewhere, and there isn't a jury in the country that would have convicted me, either. So you backed off from it, then. So okay. You had your reasons, I guess."

Again, as on that July afternoon in Rutherfurd's office, Dillon could feel a thin, painful tightness around the head, and a steady humming along with it like telephone wires in a high wind. He remained very quiet, however.

"And who else do you suppose figures that way?" he asked. "That I backed off from it? Besides somebody like you, I mean? Who else, Farrell?"

"Who else would you think?" Farrell said. It was the first time he had ever been able to show casual contempt for Johnny Dillon. He appeared to enjoy it. "Not that I meant to put it exactly that way, John. I know the kind of a spot you're in. You're getting married in a couple of weeks. So of course—"

It was a very near thing at that moment; the snap any time at all, Dillon knew. He went over and got his things from the hall closet, and was waiting out in the driveway when Rita appeared a minute or two afterward. But the conversation had shown him something. Even the clown realized what Chris Dillon's brother should have done about her; even the clown. And what had he done? What was he doing right now? Nothing.

And then Rita started in on him by declaring angrily that she couldn't understand why he had even bothered to listen to someone like Joe Farrell. He knew the kind of a loudmouth Farrell was; what he'd do. Everybody in the family knew. Why had Dillon been foolish enough to lose his head then?

"But I could listen to you," he told her. "You knew how to fix everything up—get married." He snatched for a cigarette violently. "Only where the hell was I when that kid was screaming for me? You heard Rutherfurd. Johnny, Johnny! What was I worrying about? You think I'm ever going to forget that?"

"I don't know if you can," she said, not quite steadily, "or if you won't. But I do know that you can't go on like this, Johnny. You've got to stop it. Do you want me to go back to the apartment with you, and make some coffee, and try to discuss this thing calmly and sensibly, like two adult humans? Would you like that?"

And of course that gave him the chance to hit back savagely at her, curling his lips—or perhaps at himself.

"Now that's a goddam clever idea," he said. "You could call Mamma, I suppose, and tell her you were staying up at Loretta's tonight. God Almighty! You're even worse than the rest of them. You know all the answers for Johnny Dillon, don't you?"

"Oh, I'm a clever girl," she announced bitterly. "And a very tired one, Johnny. I've had all of this I can take. Don't you understand that you hurt me very much that night, and that I was trying to hurt you? The thing happened to Chris, that's all. It wasn't your fault, and you can't help it now. Nobody can. And don't we matter a little bit? Why do you have to keep on torturing me all the time, and accusing yourself?"

"Of course," he said. "Forget it. Forget her. Well, I won't, Rita. I can't. And he isn't going to get away with what he did, no matter what. I've made up my mind!"

"Then maybe I have, too," Rita said, beginning to fuss around at the pocketbook in her lap with quick, shaky fingers. "You're doing everything that you can to make yourself into a brute savage about that man. I've tried my best for you. I've tried everything—and I was just about your last chance to pull yourself out of it, Johnny. But now you're turning on me, too. You can't stand me around any more. The way you act lately, even the way you look at me . . . I only wanted to fix you some coffee tonight, that's all, so I didn't quite deserve that remark about Mamma, Johnny. You know I didn't."

And he did know. But something—the dark brother, perhaps—would not let him admit that he knew.

"I only want people to stop pushing me," he declared breathlessly. "Is that a crime? Only I can't let him get away with it. How can I? I've got to live with myself, Rita."

"Then go ahead," she said quietly. "I'm through fighting, Johnny. I don't think it's much use any more. But I want a decent life for myself, and a decent husband, and the only thing you can think of is to go up there and beat him almost to death if he gets off; maim him, cripple him. Then you'll be all man, won't you? Or you will be for somebody like Joe Farrell. But remember this. Whatever you intend to do to him, whatever's going to satisfy you now, you'll be doing something a lot worse to yourself, and I mean that. It won't be any good for us then. We'll be all finished. You're going to be as dead as poor little Chris to me. That's all I have to say about this. If you do go up there again, if you've made up your mind, then don't you ever come back, Johnny. Not to me."

And there was no question about Rita meaning it. Plain fact, Dillon understood; cards on the table. And yet, it came to him, if he was ready to accept this last ultimatum from her, he would indeed have achieved a complete freedom of action for himself. Then no one else would be involved if action became imperative on his part, not even Rita. He would have lost Rita. Beat that man, she had remarked contemptuously; cripple him. But perhaps she did not know Johnny Dillon quite so well as she imagined she did. There was another thought in mind now than beating or crippling. An eye for an eye, as the Bible had it; a tooth for a tooth. They would see.

And they did see, rather shortly afterward. When he got home from the precinct Thursday night, Rutherfurd called him with even worse news. A new and surprising witness had now pushed himself forward. And he was a witness, it developed, who was ready to deny Willie Neale's story from beginning to end.

"Fellow named Rene Le Tendre," Rutherfurd growled. "Runs a place in town called Frenchy's Dugout, around on Bridge Street, and what he claims now is that he saw a car in Mountainview Park that night because he was up there himself at the time, but that it wasn't a gray Cadillac but a gray Buick, and that it wasn't Roy Vinson driving it. Now if that story holds up, we're not going to have much of a case left. We've got a little thinking to do, Johnny."

But it did not seem to Chris Dillon's brother that he had any thinking at all to do. As expected, he was telling himself; the wires being pulled. Rene the Tender. . . . Funny name. But now there were two of them up there. There was the one who had done the thing, and the other one who was deliberately helping him to get away with it. Which was worse?

"Then why didn't he give you this story of his last July?" he asked Rutherfurd. "Why the delay, Frank?"

"Oh, there's an excuse," Rutherfurd said. "Plausible enough, too. He's a married man, and he says he was waiting there for a married woman; so naturally, to protect the woman's good name, he hung back until his conscience began bothering him. Well, I've known him for twenty years, Johnny, and I never suspected he had one before. Not Frenchy Le Tendre."

"Then how about the woman?" Dillon asked him, very calm and quiet, of course; no excitement at all. "What's her story?"

"Well," Rutherfurd admitted reluctantly, "she tells me she did have a date with Frenchy that night, only she never kept it. Her mother got sick over in Tupper Lake. And of course Frenchy claims that he was still waiting for her at eleven o'clock, when he saw this other car drive up. He's pretty sure that it was a Buick, though not positive; but he's absolutely sure that it wasn't a Cadillac. Then the driver got out to look at one of his back tires, and Frenchy could see that it wasn't Roy Vinson. He saw the girl in the car, too. He remembers the yellow raincoat.

"But he didn't pay too much attention to the man, or to the license number. If he had, according to Frenchy, he'd have come forward right away with the correct information for us. As it was, however, he knew that he couldn't identify the man, not having got a real good look at him, only that he was a lot too short to be Vinson, or even the car; so what help would he have been? He just knows that the man couldn't have been Vinson by any stretch of the imagination, and that's all."

Yes, Dillon told himself. That was all. Le Tendre would be very sure about the driver, ready to swear to him, in fact; but nothing else. And of course if he could have identified the man, or the car, he would have found himself in a good deal of trouble with Frank Rutherfurd because he had kept quiet for so long. They were clever enough to be figuring on all the angles up there, with no loose ends to pull out suddenly, and start the whole thing falling apart. They had put it together tight as a drum. And they imagined that Chris Dillon's brother was going to let them get away with it? He got a cigarette out of his pocket, and reached for matches.

"What else did he see, Frank? Anything at all?"

"Just the necessary," Rutherfurd said. "Nothing else. He drove off about five minutes after eleven, when he decided that his date wasn't going to show up, and he claims that there was no commotion at all then in the other car. Pretty nice timing, isn't it? He didn't know anything had happened until the next morning, and then his lady friend begged him to keep quiet about it. She didn't want to get involved in the thing. Now the way it looks at this minute, a jury would have to believe Le Tendre, or believe Willie Neale, and I think I've told you about Willie. They'd get him all confused on the stand in two seconds, Johnny. He wouldn't know what he had seen, or what he hadn't seen. It's going to be pretty tricky for us."

And it would be, Dillon realized. A glib, sure witness, probably well coached, against a timid, honest and bewildered one, with every statement that Willie Neale could make contradicted forcefully and immediately. So there it was. They were just about finished trying the thing Rutherfurd's way. Johnny Dillon's, however?

"Well, I've got to hand it to them," he remarked evenly. Was he relieved, however? It seemed to him that he was. No hesitation any more; no sitting around any more; just direct physical action. But very good, again. By this time John Patrick Dillon felt himself to be altogether ready for it. "They're working it pretty neat, Frank. But what kind of a fellow is this Frenchy Le Tendre? You think he might have been slipped a little something under the pillow for himself?"

"Now that I wouldn't be prepared to say," Rutherfurd told him cautiously, the very caution admitting it. "All brag and bluster, Johnny; but by God he's going to have the fear of hell thrown into him in the next day or two. And I've got a certain idea in my head about this thing, so just let me work on it for a couple of days up here. We're not through yet, remember. We'll keep in touch."

"Right," Dillon agreed—quiet as quiet now, flat as flat. "You do that, Frank. I'll want to know."

Then he called Loretta, and told her.

"Well, I expected something like this," she declared angrily. "I don't know what was the matter with you for the last couple of months, Johnny. You just wouldn't go up there again; you just wouldn't do anything at all. And Joe warned you, too. You let it drag on too long."

"What?" Dillon said. So there would be Number One now, he was advising himself, and Number Two; a little different, consequently. A certain amount of thought would be needed. "But I was doing something," he said. "I was getting married in two weeks. I thought you heard, Lorry. You got the invitation, didn't you?"

"Now, Johnny," Loretta said. She probably remembered that soft, even tone in him, and the expression with it. "Call Rita, why don't you? Talk to her about this. Then we'll get together tomorrow night up here, the whole family, and make up our minds about it. Joe

67

could help us a lot, I think. His brother Walter's a lawyer."

"Fine," Dillon said. "That's it, Lorry." But there seemed to be a twisted humor about the suggestion that Joe Farrell could give him some ideas now, and he felt that he grinned slightly. "You bet," he told her. "We'll talk it over, all right, and be sure Joe's around. But look. I have to go out to Chicago tomorrow morning with Ted Larkin. We're picking up a couple of fugitives out there, and I don't think that we'll get back till Saturday night, or maybe Sunday morning. In the meantime, though, I'll try to figure out what we can do about this. I'll call you the minute I get in, Lorry. I promise."

So there was the first step of all for Chris Dillon's brother, and nothing complicated or difficult about it. It was Thursday night now, he reminded himself, and two days up in Hazard Lake would be quite long enough for him, if he could only make them two free and clear days, with no interruptions from anyone. Time to get going on it now.

And he got going. He pulled his big suitcase out of the closet, and began packing. In ten minutes or so the phone rang, but he did not answer it. He was otherwise occupied. He decided that it was Rita, perhaps, because of course she and Loretta would have talked it all over between themselves by this time; but let her call. Two of them up there now, and both equally culpable. Which first?

He began thinking coldly and carefully about that part, and about what he would need in a place like Hazard Lake at this time of year. First his revolver, of course, and then maybe his hunting rifle. And what else?

He still felt calm, sensible and alert. But then, once the dark brother had been given full rein, he turned out to be a pretty good organizer. John Patrick Dillon might have overlooked a few necessary items. The dark brother did not. He remembered to pack heavy woolen underwear, gloves, a sweater, a flashlight and a couple of flannel shirts. Then last of all he got Dillon's hunting rifle out of the closet, a fine, thoroughly accurate weapon, a present from Rita last Christmas, and inspected it.

The rifle would of course permit him a longer and even more dependable range up there, since Detective Dillon was an excellent shot with it, as he was with the service revolver. Up on the shelf, in fact, were a couple of marksman's medals, and once he had gone out to the West Coast with the police rifle team. So there would be very little difficulty about that part. At any reasonable distance he could expect to hit what he wanted to hit, and dead center; Dillon the sharpshooter. But which first?

He decided, when his packing had been all finished, that he would be pretty foolish to make up his mind about who was going to be Number One for him, and who Number Two. He would have to hold up on that now, look over the ground first. Yet Hazard Lake was a pretty small town, and the news about Number One, whichever it turned out to be, would be common knowledge almost as soon as Detective Dillon had attended to him. So he would have to be very quick in regard to Number Two, with Rutherfurd on the alert. He would have to take care of him in the shortest possible time interval following Number One, who would of course present no serious problem; not even Frank Rutherfurd aware and suspicious yet. Could he manage them both at almost the same time, perhaps?

He began thinking about that, and with a good sense of purpose and dedication in him. He was, after all, a trained specialist in these matters. So why couldn't he manage them? He had only to inspect the ground for himself, set up a tight, second-by-second schedule for them, and determine on the particular method of attack to be used; then it would be very difficult, indeed, to set up any adequate defense against Dillon the sharp-shooter. Very good, again. No time must be wasted. Number One; Number Two; and *finie la guerre.*

He called Rita. He wanted no suspicion about him-self, not from any quarter, and therefore he gave her Rutherfurd's big news, which she appeared to have known from Loretta already, and explained about his trip out to Chicago tomorrow morning.

"But I'll try to call you after I get out there," he told her, deciding he would, too, because Rita might know him just a little better than Loretta did, although even Rita could not say whether a long distance call was coming through to her from Chicago or Hazard Lake with the new dialing system—or coming from around the corner, for that matter. "I'll want to talk to you, hon. I'm still pretty numb about this. Do I sound all right? Rutherfurd said that they might have to drop the whole case up there, with this fellow Le Tendre pop-ping up. I wish you were here with me right now, Rita. I feel that I'd like to talk to someone."

"Then I'll drive over," Rita said. "It's still only half past eight, Johnny. I can pick up Loretta, too. We'll be there in about an hour, the two of us."

But that was a little too much conviction from him. He permitted the dark brother to twist out plausibly.

"Oh, I'll be all right," he said. "Rutherfurd knows what he's doing up there. And then if I start talking to you and Loretta about this, I won't sleep for the whole rest of the night, hon. I better not. Let me call you from Chicago tomorrow night."

"Then all right," Rita said, after a brief, anxious hesi-tation about it. "I don't want you to get all worked up,

Johnny. Do you have any of those sleeping pills I gave you?"

"Took two of them already," he lied. "I had to, Rita. I just seemed to be getting jittery as hell all of a sudden. Maybe I ought to fix a little hot milk for myself, and turn in."

"I think I would," Rita said. "That's the best thing. And don't forget to call me tomorrow afternoon, Johnny. I'll be home about five-thirty."

Which attended to Rita. After that he made a pot of strong black coffee out in the kitchen, feeling that everything had at last been settled for him, or almost everything. There was just one other small point to be decided. Dillon the sharpshooter could pay off Number One and Number Two now like knocking over a couple of wooden ducks in some Coney Island shooting gallery—if he was that kind of a man. Was he? You had to be a certain type to plan and execute something like this in cold blood, and what type was John Patrick Dillon? Had he ever attempted to find out before?

He attempted it now, at any rate. During the hours that followed he smoked cigarette after cigarette out in the kitchen; made more coffee; and remembered everybody who would have to be involved now, one way or another, in what he planned, whether he wanted them involved or not—of Rita, dead Chrissy, the sisters, Frank Rutherfurd. At times in his relationship and responsibility to all those people he would feel like Detective Dillon even yet; but at other times, when the pendulum swung in the other direction, he would know himself to be the dark brother in true fact.

He was not too sure about who he was when one o'clock came, and two, and then three; but at ten minutes of four he managed to get through to the other side finally. He had settled the last question for himself. He knew then the kind of man that John Patrick Dillon was; what he could do, and what he couldn't do. And he made himself face up to the answer he got. They were not walking off scot free from this thing. He could not let them do that, and so, as Detective Dillon, there was only one possible way in which he could take action against them. Then it would have to be done in that way. But could he accept the fact that Detective Dillon would have to go pretty far over the line in order to do it?

Very soon it seemed evident that he could, and after that there were no more questions for him. He lay down on the living room couch, very tired after a rather long night of it, and yet oddly relieved also. He left a small lamp on, and pulled an afghan over himself. From then on, until eight o'clock Friday morning, he went sound asleep.

CHAPTER 4

And everything was still firm and decided in him when he got up at that time—what kind of man he was; what he could do, what he couldn't do. There were no more questions to be answered. There was only one way to do the thing now as Detective Dillon. He had no choice. And so he proceeded to do it in that way.

He dressed warmly, then—heavy underwear, suede windbreaker, leather hunting cap, thick sheepskin coat —and telephoned his precinct to place Detective Dillon on sick report. That seemed to close up the last hole behind him. There should be no question now from any quarter as to his whereabouts for the next couple of days. The whole weekend lay free. He had only to use it in the right way. He locked the suitcase, put the hunting rifle under his arm and left the apartment. On the stairs going down he met old Mr. Foley from the second floor, coming in with a bottle of milk and a bag of breakfast rolls. A little hunting trip? Mr. Foley inquired.

"That's it," Dillon said. "A little hunting trip, Mr. Foley. I'm using up a couple of free days."

"Ah, you're a wise man," Mr. Foley said. "There'll be damned small chance for anything like that when the new regime starts putting its foot down; and it will, Johnny. There's not a one of them but begin to tighten the reins, once the harness is on. When's the big event coming off? Sometime this month, did the wife tell me?"

"I guess that's what we were figuring on," Dillon agreed with him. "But maybe you never know, Mr. Foley."

"Now what are you saying?" Mr. Foley demanded. "Easy on, Johnny. We all have a bit of natural panic in us at the last moment. I did myself, forty-two years ago. But watch the weather outside. I hear they're expecting a little snow over the weekend."

Up in Hazard Lake, however, there must have been snow for two or three months now. Was he fully prepared for it? He thought again about that while getting his car from the garage, and then attended to several other small details. In a liquor store he bought a pint of brandy; in the corner delicatessen he bought enough canned goods for two people over the weekend; and last of all he stopped at his neighborhood bank and withdrew his whole savings account in cash. It came to a little over fourteen hundred and twenty dollars.

Perhaps he would not need all of that, but perhaps he would; impossible to say yet. But afterward he did not intend to run, he promised himself. It would be silly to try, for that matter. Frank Rutherfurd would know immediately who had done the thing. Everybody would. But that was all right with Dillon; fine, even. He wanted them to know. That was part of the way. The act would have to be presented as a simple and justified act, so that by this time tomorrow or Sunday Detective Dillon would be considered beyond the pale, and no way back, either. Otherwise the thing would not go. He knew what he had to do for Chris; what he owed her. Time to move now.

So he did move, the sense of purpose and dedication remaining in him. Around Rhinebeck he saw the first immaculate glitter of fresh snow off in the woods, and from then on it crept in closer and closer to the car with each mile. Very soon there were splotches of dark gray ice on the road, and he could see tree branches glittering in the feeble January sunlight as if with a coating of brittle silver paint spread over them. About eleven o'clock it snowed for half an hour or so, and then stopped. The skies remained dark and ominous, however, from then on.

Yet he made excellent time on the ride up. He had hour after hour to think about the right way to do it with Number One and Number Two, and he did think, no Rita with him today, and not much traffic to bother him. It seemed to him that everything was in place, finally; he settled a lot of small details, had a cup of coffee outside Albany for himself and was out on the road again in half an hour.

It began to get very cold after Albany. The air acquired a hard, irony tang, and the outside thermometer at a Schroon Lake gas station showed him that it was already six degrees below zero, at two in the afternoon. And of course there was snow everywhere in this mountain country. Banks of it had been plowed over to each side of the road, and here and there he passed a town sand truck. It was almost the only traffic he met. He saw only a few people in the towns, all well muffled;

the roadside restaurants and stands had been closed up; and sometimes for ten or fifteen minutes he would find himself all alone in a new and rather ominous world for Dillon the city man, frozen peaks and ridges all around, a few lazily drifting white flakes in the air, and bare, twisted trees standing up against the snow on each side of him like dead wood.

Yet he pushed on doggedly, car windows frosting up, car heater not much good any more. And it was very cold, all right; achingly cold. More flurries of snow fell. The sky became darker and heavier up ahead, and ugly thick clouds boiled up over gaunt ridges. But in North Falls there were several very stylish motels, all glass and glitter for the ski trade, on the outskirts of town, and he chose the biggest and fanciest one. There would be more guests there, and so less attention paid to one in particular. He rented the last individual cabin out along the lake front, and registered as Mr. and Mrs. James Foley, and Mr. and Mrs. Edward Foley, of Brooklyn, New York. The rest of them would be in later tonight, he told the desk clerk. They were driving up in another car.

In the town proper he made a few additional purchases; women's things. Lights were coming on in the village then, and back at the motel it was almost full dark against the backdrop of somber Adirondack woods. But it seemed to him that he had managed everything well enough. He messed up the beds and bathrooms in the double cabin as if four careless people on holiday had been using them, leaving a nightgown and a pair of pajamas in one bedroom, and unpacking his suitcase in the other. Then he put the canned goods into his suitcase, locked it and shoved it way back on the closet shelf.

No one paid any attention to him when he came back

to the cabin, or when he left it. The rifle was still in his car trunk. The service revolver was still available in his belt holster. In one pocket of his overcoat he carried the flashlight, and in the other his pint bottle of brandy. He decided that he was just about ready then; a few minutes before five Friday afternoon. He had arranged a free weekend for himself, in Detective Dillon's opinion.

On the last fifteen miles of his ride, over to Hazard Lake, it seemed to him that if anything went wrong now, and very probably it would, Detective Dillon knew from bitter professional experience, that at least he would have a pretty good cover for himself in Mr. and Mrs. James Foley, and Mr. and Mrs. Edward Foley. When the thing started, Rutherfurd in all likelihood would check the motels in and around Hazard Lake for a single man answering Dillon's description; but the hunting cap, a pair of dark glasses which he had also bought in North Falls, and the openly registered party of four people might well throw Rutherfurd off for a while. Maybe it would be a very short while; but a very short while, granted a minimum of luck from now on, would be all that Dillon would need. He was pretty sure that he had established a good base of operations for himself. Now for the rest of it, and for that second-by-second schedule he had to set up, it was necessary to look over the field of action sharply and carefully.

He did that. At twenty minutes past five he was driving past Jack Riley's King of the North Snack Bar, and found it all shuttered up for the winter, no cars in the parking area, a couple of feet of snow on the roof, and silvery long icicles glittering against the sudden flash of his headlights from the malted milk and hot dog signs. Just beyond was the Hazard Lake auto graveyard, where he saw hundreds and hundreds of old wrecks arranged listlessly on an open field, then a gas station on his left, and what appeared to be a parochial school over on a low hill to the right.

He stopped at the gas station. C. Dooley, Prop., a big yellow and black sign told him; Poor Old Charley's—Give Him a Hand Can't You? Then the office door opened, and Poor Old Charley appeared in person, a jaunty little clothespin of a man with a sallow, wizened face, a freckled and not too clean-looking complexion and foxily inquisitive brown eyes. He filled the gas tank for Dillon, checked the oil and the anti-freeze and cleaned off the windshield.

"But you notice them back tires?" he demanded, appearing very concerned about them. "Smooth as a baby's butt, fella. You're going to be skidding all over the road by tomorrow morning if we get any more snow around here, and the paper says we're due for ten or twelve inches tonight. Why don't you let me fix you up with a couple of nice new snow caps? Nothing like them in this climate, buddy. And I'll toss in the second one at half price this week. What the hell—everybody around here is getting the best of Poor Old Charley. How about it, hah?"

It seemed a sensible precaution to Dillon, even this late. Quick and dependable transportation was going to be a vital necessity up here for the next day or two, and he should have remembered himself about snow tires. They might be extremely important. So he haggled a bit with Poor Old Charley for the appearance of it, struck the bargain with him and then consulted the office telephone book while the tires were being put on.

One address, 147 Lake Avenue, he still remembered from last summer, but he found a Frenchy's Dugout listed at 22 Bridge Street, and a Rene Le Tendre on

Forestville Road, no number. It appeared simple enough.

"Forestville Road?" Dooley chirped. He had a high, whiny voice, immensely wise and knowing. It suited his actions. "Well, sure I know. Know this whole goddam town like a book, buddy. But who you looking for out there? Then I could tell you."

It should have been the one obviously expected question by Detective Dillon, and yet he found himself not quite ready for it.

"I don't know," he said, deciding that the best thing would be to match Dooley in kind. "I'm a bank examiner. They got me checking all the snow banks around here, Charley. You ask a hell of a lot of questions, don't you?"

"Say, that's pretty good," Dooley said, squatting down now at the back of the car, and spinning off the wheel bolts neatly and briskly with a tire spanner. "Checking the snow banks, hah? Well, you're sure going to find a lot of frozen assets up in this neck of the woods, buddy. Sit down over there. Take a load off your feet. Where you from?"

"Red Bank, New Jersey," Dillon said. "I'll show you my passport. Get busy on the tires, will you?"

"Ten minutes," Dooley promised. "You like girlie magazines? There's a stack in the office."

"Thanks," Dillon said. "I'm not old enough, Charley. Is it always this cold up here?"

"Come around in February," Dooley said. "Wow! You know they can't bury a guy this time of year. Ground frozen. They lean him up against a barn somewhere, and leave him standing. He don't mind."

"That's what you think," Dillon said. His head ached a little, and that cruddy stomach of his bothered him. Only coffee all day, he remembered. Yet it wasn't bad talking to Poor Old Charley. It eased the tension a little. "I've heard a complaint here and there," he said. "The word gets around, Charley. You don't lean them right."

"Well, you can't hang them up," Charley said. "That wouldn't look good, buddy. Draws the neck muscles. How's your spare? You want to keep one of these for yourself?"

"Whatever you think," Dillon said. "Look at it."

So Charley took the keys out of the ignition switch, and opened the trunk. It was another very careless mistake by Detective Dillon. He had forgotten that the hunting rifle was on the floor of the trunk, and in plain sight.

"Say," Dooley said. He picked it up cockily, and hefted it. "That's a nice gun. You hunt, buddy?"

"Now and then," Dillon said, savagely annoyed with himself this time. "Anything else you'd like to know about me? You're still asking questions, Charley."

"That right?" Dooley said. He remained chipper as ever, putting the rifle down. "I only meant the season's all over, buddy. You better watch yourself. Them troopers pull you over to the side of the road once in a while, and make you open the trunk for them. Around here a lot of guys go out shining deer at night. Of course a lot of them get caught, too."

"I'll try to remember," Dillon said, the head aching a little more. He wasn't doing quite so well as he had thought he would; losing the touch. And he had promised to call Rita, hadn't he? It was a quarter of six. He got up. "Do you have a pay phone around, Charley?"

"Out in the office," Dooley said, clanging away briskly. "Calling home, buddy? Calling the Bronx?"

"What?" Detective Dillon said. He turned back grimly, and then realized—his license plates. Poor Old Charley didn't miss very much. All this was a pretty poor start for Number One and Number Two. Where were his brains?

He went on into the office, and called Rita after getting some change out of his pocket. But there was a small difficulty there, also. The circuits were busy, and when the operator got him back ten minutes later he was washing his hands in the station restroom, and Dooley had to rap on the door for him.

Now everything appeared to be going wrong. Perhaps the operator had said something to Rita about Hazard Lake, but while he was groping desperately for an excuse about that, it turned out to be all right. The operator had said nothing, apparently. Rita's first question was about how he felt, and her second what the weather in Chicago was like.

"Well, not too bad," Dillon told her, sweating a bit. He was making mistake after mistake now, and he hadn't even started the thing. He would have to pick up. "Like New York, I guess. But there's some kind of trouble about the extradition papers, and I don't know whether or not I'll be able to get home before Monday. Don't expect me until I call, Rita. It's all fouled up out here."

"Then get a good rest over the weekend," she said. "I know you sounded all right when I talked to you last night, Johnny, but I don't think you were, actually. I was worried about you."

A good rest over the weekend, Dillon thought. He cleared his throat, and felt something weak, shaky and traitorous take over in him.

"I'll be all right," he said. "Don't worry about that. I just called because I want you to know how I feel about you, and how I always will, Rita. Goodbye now."

"Wait a minute," she said anxiously. "Johnny! Are you sure—"

He hung up on her, having managed about all that he could with Rita, and apparently with himself. He was still standing with his shoulders against the wall, thinking about Rita, when Charley Dooley came strutting out of the work area.

"You know something?" Poor Old Charley demanded, giving him another shrewdly inquisitive scrutiny. "You look like you just lost your last friend, buddy. Who caved the roof in?"

"Kind of a long story," Dillon said. He knew that Rita would stick to him to the bitter end, and he didn't want that. There was very little that Detective Dillon, once over the line, could offer to her. Turn back, then, while he still had a chance to turn back? He felt his jaws clamping. "And I notice you're still asking questions," he said. "You seem to have the habit, Charley. How much do I owe you?"

"Well, let's see," Dooley said, starting off with a grand flourish on one of his billheads. "Gas, oil, quart of antifreeze, two snowcaps—and of course my own personal labor charge, buddy. That comes to forty-six dollars and eighty-four cents, all told. You got a credit card?"

"Only the best," Dillon said, taking a fifty-dollar bill out of his wallet, and passing it over, but remembering to place one palm over his department shield. "Uncle Sam's old reliable, Charley. Keep the change."

"Well, say," Poor Old Charley said. "Don't mind if I do, buddy. Thanks. You know I like your style, somehow. You from anywhere around Jerome Avenue, kid? That's where I used to hang out. Then of course I had to get the old T.B. twenty-five years ago, and come up here, and now I'm stuck in the dump. But you know I always had luck like that. Now all you have to do is take a couple of pills for it, and they fix you up in two weeks. What the hell, though—maybe I only have half of one lung left, but they ain't stopping me with the old viggerish, kid. Drop in again, hah? Nice talking to you."

"Right," Dillon said, and managed to grin stiffly. "Take it easy, Charley. When I get back to Jerome Avenue, I'll pass the word that you're knocking them dead up here."

Poor Old Charley followed him out to the car.

"Wisht I was," he said, something wistful and almost likable in him now. "I suppose I can't kick, though. What the hell. I live upstairs, buddy; me and the cat. How old do you think I am?"

"Forty?" Dillon said, shading it a little, as he knew was expected of him. "Forty-two, Charley?"

Dooley cackled.

"Fifty-four," he said. "Fifty-four, kid. Wouldn't believe it, hah? Nobody does. The easy life, I guess. Nothing like it. Once in a while I hire one of these country broads for a little light housekeeping, and then boot her to hell out. There's always another one. You staying over in town tonight? Maybe we could do something."

"I'll write you a special delivery letter," Dillon told him; "when I know. Thanks a lot, Charley. Where did you say the Forestville Road was?"

It proved to be over on the other side of Hazard Lake, a mile or two back of the Town Hall. He had to drive out to the end of Franklin Avenue first, beyond the last street light, and then turn left at a big dairy farm. On Forestville Road itself he passed only one or two wooden shacks, with the windows gone, and the doors caved in, and then his headlights picked up the name Le Tendre on an R.F.D. mailbox.

The house itself was a two-story frame affair, set well back from the road, and with a neglected barn behind it. A pile of fireplace logs, four or five feet high, had been stacked up under an adjoining leanto, and on all sides of the house, save where it faced the road from an old-fashioned front porch, the somber Adirondack woods closed it in. The approach to it, Dillon noted, would prove very simple. There was no light showing in any of the windows, and no car in the driveway.

It seemed to him an excellent starting point, with no close neighbors this far from town, and the woods on three sides. Probably it would offer a much safer opening move for him than 147 Lake Avenue. But Number Two? There was the time element to be considered now. How far would it measure off on his car speedometer from Forestville Road to the Mrs. Roy Vinson residence?

He tested it. Back on Franklin Avenue he asked directions from a small boy, which seemed safe enough to him, drove back to the Town Hall again, turned to his right from there, but just a little, and found a broad thoroughfare curving around on the east side of the lake as the road to North Falls curved around on the opposite side. It was a much better neighborhood than Forestville Road, with big, neatly painted wooden homes, all of them well tended, and 147 Lake Avenue proved to be one of the biggest and most imposing of all. The house must have contained at least ten or twelve rooms, with a steeply pitched roof, and an attic over the second floor that had four oversized dormer windows facing the road. The driveway and the front steps had been shoveled off, and a comfortable plume of gray smoke drifted up from the chimney. Lights were showing on the first floor, and a glistening gray Cadillac was parked in front of a three-car wooden garage to the rear.

A gray Cadillac, Dillon told himself; probably the same car Willie Neale had seen that night up in Mountainview Park. And he knew now that it was just a mile and eight tenths between Number One and Number Two, which meant no more that three or four minutes of driving time, even in very bad weather. It could be done then, despite Rutherfurd, and done in exactly the way Detective Dillon had decided to do it last night; the right way. Number One, with the conditions prevailing, would be Frenchy Le Tendre; Number Two the other fellow. He drove all the way out on Lake Avenue, to where it curved in to the North Falls Road two miles from town, and that also was very good. Give him any luck at all either tonight or tomorrow night, and he should be back in that comfortable double cabin of his, everything in hand, no more than half an hour after he had started the thing off with Number One.

It was such excellent progress for him that he began to feel a bit light-headed. Going too well, maybe? But he remembered the old gambling adage—pull in when you're behind, spread out when you're ahead; and so he drove back to Main Street again, and parked his car in a supermarket lot just across from the Seneca movie house.

There was a lot of traffic around on the streets, and a lot of people. But of course. Friday night; weekend shopping to do, and a big snowstorm to beat. He got out of the car, dark glasses on now, hunting cap well down in case of a chance meeting with Frank Rutherfurd, and found Bridge Street.

It crossed Main on the other side of the Hazard House, and number 22 was about halfway along in the block. On the street level was a small jewelry store. Under it, reached by a flight of rickety wooden steps, was Frenchy's Dugout. A narrow creek ran under Bridge Street at this point, and at the foot of the stairway he found a long, glassed-in porch, overlooking the creek, that was probably very pleasant in the summer months.

But now there was no longer any outdoor service available. All the chairs and tables had been jumbled together at the far end, and a dim storm entry led off to the bar proper.

It did not seem to him a very busy or prosperous bar, which was another nail in the barrelhead. At this time of year, with no summer trade to be expected until June or July, Rene the Tender might have found himself in need of a little ready cash. Very good, again; the whole thing was fitting together neatly by this time. In the bar itself there were only two customers, even at the height of the cocktail hour, and another man, perhaps Frenchy in person, who was leaning with one elbow up on top of the cash register, and talking to them.

He was a short, burly man with black hair that was getting a bit thin in front, a round, rather pale face, and an air of determined masculine vigor and assurance about him. But perhaps, Dillon told himself, the vigor and assurance were just a little too obvious. What had Rutherfurd said? All brag and bluster. They would soon know.

The burly man served him a Scotch and plain water, rang up seventy-five cents on the cash register and went back to his friends. Then the phone rang in the pay booth, and one of the customers answered it. "Yeah," he said. "Right here. Hey, Frenchy."

So the identification was made. Le Tendre came around from behind the bar, walking with what he must have considered just the right touch of manly truculence, and closed the booth door after himself. The two male customers began murmuring together.

"Who was that?" one of them said. "Art Palmer's wife? He's been playing her a long time, hasn't he? I mean for Frenchy."

"Yeah, quite a while," the other one said. "Since last summer, I guess, when his wife left him and went back to her mother's up in Montreal with the three kids. I guess we all like it pretty good, but that Frenchman loves it. Doris Palmer isn't too bad, though. I wouldn't mind it myself. You been over to Jack O'Neill's place in Tupper lately? How is Jack?"

So it had been a very good thing, indeed, for Chris Dillon's brother to keep pushing his luck. He knew Frenchy in person now, no mistake possible about him, and he had learned another important detail about Forestville Road—the wife gone, the children gone; Frenchy all alone out there. After that he made only one more stop in town for himself, Mountainview Park. He asked directions for it at a big gas station back on Main Street.

It was out on the North Falls Road, past Dooley's place and the parochial school, past the auto graveyard. He had to drive back on a dirt road into the woods, then up a hill, where the snow tires helped him a lot, and then curve around once more, at the top of the ridge, to the state highway. His headlights picked out a few wooden tables and benches, all desolately snow covered, half a dozen stone fireplaces, a parking area and just beyond a circular terrace or lookout point.

There was a low stone wall running around the edge, about knee high. Probably somewhere along here, Dillon told himself. Johnny, Johnny. . . . Under him a car came racing around the turn from North Falls, and he could see the highway seventy or eighty feet down, and even the projecting hillside rock Rutherfurd had mentioned to him last summer. Well, he thought quietly, no Johnny had been around for her last July, busy with other things. He was around for her now, however. Number One and Number Two had not got away with it quite yet.

The car flashed by, and it seemed to get a lot darker and quieter than before in Mountainview Park. He could see only a very thin strip of dark blue sky over to the east, with a few early stars visible, and then the other way, clustered around the tip end of Hazard Lake, the illuminated clock on the Town Hall building, with a few other lights looking tiny and scattered behind it on Franklin Avenue. Everywhere else, there was frozen darkness and desolation, deep winter woods, aching stillness. But darkness and desolation, it came to him, was where the dark brother lived, native habitat; and he would have to keep the dark brother very carefully in hand tonight. He had to manage this thing in the right way for Chris. He owed her that much. Very soon now Detective Dillon would be over the line. Well . . .

He drove back again to North Falls, and had supper. But remembering in time that it was Friday night, he ordered the clam chowder and the broiled mackerel for himself. Then he couldn't seem to eat very much. The greasy smell and taste of the fish sickened him, but he did manage to get down a slice of bread and butter, some canned peas, a spoonful of the mashed potatoes and some coffee and pie afterward. Often in his line of work he had been required to make snap judgments about people, and now while finishing the coffee he made one about Frenchy Le Tendre which completely agreed with Frank Rutherfurd's estimate of the man. It was the most vital part of his design, and now he was satisfied with it. He decided to start the wheels turning.

There was a pay booth in the restaurant, and he used it to call Frenchy's Dugout back in Hazard Lake.

"Frenchy?" he demanded, when that toughly aggressive masculine voice barked out at him from the other booth. "I wondered if you'd give me a little information about something. You ever go to church, Frenchy?"

There was a slight, rather bewildered pause after that, but Dillon could picture the liquid black eyes beginning to flicker around uneasily. The voice, how-ever, got even louder and more aggressive.

"Well, who the hell wants to know?" Frenchy said. "Who's so interested, hah? This Art Palmer? Well, listen here, wise guy. You ain't scaring anybody. And if you ever lay a finger on Doris again—"

"Take a guess," Dillon advised softly. "It isn't Art Palmer, though. Name of Dillon mean anything to you? Think it over. And then go to church, Frenchy. Go to confession, even. I would. You don't have much time."

He hung up, went back to his double cabin, where everything looked exactly as he had left it earlier, and lay down there until eleven o'clock. That seemed to him about the right time—not too early now, and not too late either. It was beginning to snow heavily when he came out, and he was again grateful to Poor Old Charley for that suggestion about the snow tires; his friend from Jerome Avenue, he remembered. At half past eleven, back in Hazard Lake again, he stopped in a place called Dewdrop's Tavern on Main Street and called the Vinson house.

There was no answer.

He took thought about that. The sooner the better, he had decided by this time; even tonight if possible, granted that he could line up Number One and then Number Two properly. But was Vinson out of the house tonight? Was Vinson asleep? It became neces-sary to investigate that, and after sufficient thought he remembered Rutherfurd telling him that the hotel bar was a great hangout for Number Two.

He tried the bar, finding a street entrance that led directly in to the taproom. In that way he was able to avoid the hotel lobby, and a desk clerk who might just have remembered him from last summer, although Dillon could not recall anything about the desk clerk, even faintly. He wanted to take no chances, however. There would be chances enough later. So he made sure first from the entry vestibule that Frank Rutherfurd was not present in the Hazard House Sachem Room, and then entered.

There was a big mural painting over the cash register, and two bartenders on duty. Other Adirondack scenes adorned the wall over the booths, which were well filled even at this hour. The bar stools were well filled, too, in sharp contrast to Frenchy's Dugout earlier in the evening, and the jukebox was going. There were at least twenty or twenty-five customers in the place, which was another snag. Which of these people, if he was present at all, was Number Two?

But Detective Dillon was of course well versed in identifying a suspect, and of course without alerting the suspect. So he ordered a Scotch and water at the bar, left it sitting for him and walked over to a public telephone booth off the back passage. It was all very simple for him. He called the Hazard House number and got the switchboard girl; he asked for the bar; and then, by twisting his head a little, he could watch one of the bartenders stop muddling in a couple of old-fashioned glasses, dry his hands on a bar towel and reach back for the wall telephone. Now, although twenty or twenty-five feet distant, it was possible for him to both hear and observe the bartender.

"Yeah?" the bartender said. "Who did you want? Well, he was here. Just a minute now. Let me see."

He glanced over toward the wall booths, raising his right arm by way of signal, and beckoned to someone. Then Mr. Roy Vinson appeared, Number Two, and Detective Dillon discovered that he wasn't quite so cool and composed, everything in calm working order for him, as he had imagined. He hung up immediately. His right hand had begun to tremble. Also, because of the heat in the booth, and his sheepskin coat, he appeared to be sweating the least bit.

But after that there was of course no question about Number Two, either. He looked to be about twenty-three years old to Dillon—Chris had always been very much impressed by what she called really mature men—tall and husky in build, with blond hair, a neat, square jaw and neat, square features. He was wearing a yellow cashmere sweater with a soft scarf tucked in around the throat, very distinguished and becoming to him. Six foot two, Dillon told himself; at least a hundred and eighty-five pounds; and little Chris. But all right. He remained in the booth until Number Two, after announcing himself futilely into the wall phone, handed it back to the bartender and asked a question. The bartender shrugged, too, and spread out his hands. Then Number Two went back to his table, and was still sitting there when Dillon came out. He was alone. He had a pony of brandy in front of him, and a long, thin cigar, newly lit, in his right hand.

There was the usual bar mirror, which afforded Dillon the chance to study him at more length without looking toward the booth itself, and perhaps attracting his attention in that way. But anyone should have been able to tell by the eyes, Dillon found himself thinking helplessly, if they knew anything; only what had poor little Chris known? Dark gray eyes, with a man-of-the-world insolence and assurance for everyone; very thick lashes; very clear and prominent whites. He was now studying, the cigar smoke drifting lazily out of his mouth, a waitress who had put down some drinks at the next table.

She was a dark, pretty girl, not too much older than Chris, but obviously a lot smarter and more experienced. When she had finished serving, Number Two detained her by putting a hand on her arm but she detached the hand in the calmest possible manner, said something to him with the accompaniment of a bright, professional smile, and went back to the bar. After that she paid no attention at all to him. Number Two, puffing out more cigar smoke, glanced at the watch on his wrist and checked the time again by looking up at the bar clock.

Johnny, Johnny. . . . And Johnny standing here.

"Hey!" the bartender said. "What's the matter, mister? You're spilling that drink all over yourself. Watch it."

It must have been the dark brother again. Very stupid of him, Dillon realized. No emotion at all now; everything in the most precise sequence, rather, with both Number One and Number Two at last placed and identified by him. He must not spoil anything. So he left the Sachem Room, and Number Two did not even glance up at him as he went by. Number Two was still watching the waitress and sipping his brandy casually. But the eyes betrayed him again. They were not open and attractive eyes, despite the lashes. They looked out at other people, and inspected them, Dillon thought, as the other people might relate for possible pleasure or profit to Mr. Roy Vinson; but they revealed nothing. Yes, Chris must have been very much impressed by a complete man of the world like Number Two; thrilled to death. Until, at eleven o'clock one night up in Mountainview Park . . .

It was snowing much harder when he walked out of the Hazard House taproom. Now there was an inch or so on the streets, and on the parked cars along the curb. And it was turning much colder, too; a savage, penetrating cold, numbing the face after a step or two. The big circular thermometer across the street, over the offices of the Hazard Lake *Daily Enterprise*, showed him that it was now twenty-two degrees below zero. He walked down to Dewdrop's Tavern again, and called Frenchy's Dugout.

This time he was answered by a new voice from there, not the tender one's.

"Frenchy?" it said. "Well, no. No, he ain't. This is Al, the relief man. But you could try him out at his house, I guess. There wasn't a hell of a lot doing tonight, so he went home early. Who is this?"

So everything was quite ready for him. It would be tonight, Dillon decided. Fine.

"Okay," he said. "I'll try him out there. Thanks, Al."

He did not know whether he was nervous or not nervous. Now there was a numbness not altogether from the cold in him. So he had a small brandy at the bar, to steady himself, and waited fifteen minutes by the clock for Frenchy to get well settled out there on the Forestville Road. Then it was time for him to move again. The joints up here, Dewdrop's bartender told him, had to close at one o'clock, and so he would have to finish with Number One, and be back in the Sachem Room for Number Two, a little before that time.

He wanted to feel detached and dedicated again. He could not. His throat hurt him, probably from smoking too much; he had a slight headache; and of course the stomach had knotted up. When he was back in his car, he sat quiet for a moment, feeling oddly vacant in thought, with only these last few minutes for him now, on the right side of the line, the line he had never crossed before, and had never thought he could make himself cross; but there was still Johnny, Johnny to think about. So he thought about it, and got started once more.

He might have had a little trouble with the Franklin Avenue hill only for the new snow tires. Now there were slick, slippery patches of ice under the snow, where other cars had been forced to grind up spinning and skidding, inch after inch. But he made it in good fashion, keeping the Chevy in low gear, and with a light foot on the gas pedal. There was no difficulty at all once he had got to the top, and no traffic for the rest of the way, or on the Forestville Road, at this hour.

When he came to his turnoff the big dairy farm was quiet and dark, not a light anywhere. He slowed up even more then, with no help from the street lights, and the snow coming down thickly and steadily against his windshield. There was a narrow lane he had noticed this afternoon, just before he had come to the Le Tendre house, and he backed around in there, so that he would be headed out in the right direction for Franklin Avenue, and left the car motor on, but the headlights off. And now there was no question for Detective Dillon about whether he was nervous or not. He dropped the rifle when he got it out of his trunk. He dropped it again after picking it up the first time. He could feel his heart pumping.

But he knew that the thing was not to hesitate at all. Had he the flashlight? Yes. He needed it, too. The snow had tricked him. From the car there had been an illusion of soft, cozy white all around, but once away from the car he found himself in almost pitch blackness, so that he could feel the snow touch against his face with light, icy kisses, very gentle and cold and delicate, but not see it any longer. Then he found the Forestville Road again, after snapping the flashlight on, and began following it along to the Le Tendre house.

But he had moved no more than half the distance toward it when a certain thought came into his head. Wasn't there an old legal phrase about how a man had to appear in court with clean hands? He had already decided on the right way, indeed the only possible way, to have Number One and Number Two pay for Chris

Dillon; yet he could never manage the thing with clean hands. Maybe it would be all for nothing, then.

It was an altogether dismaying thought to Detective Dillon. He stopped anxiously, snapping the flashlight off, and started to think anxiously. But why? Because he was at the one critical point now, and was reaching out for any reason to back off from it, as Joe Farrell must have thought that he had been backing off from it all along? He cursed breathlessly. Well, he could finish it one way or the other, then, either as John Patrick Dillon or the dark brother. What did they deserve, anyway, the two of them? He had come this far. He would go on!

And he did go on. Soon afterward he saw the Le Tendre mailbox tilted out to him, and behind it, through all the thickly falling snow in between, a dim, fuzzy glow from the house itself. After that he slipped the flashlight back in his pocket, fully oriented now, and kept the edge of woods on his right.

Off the road, however, the snow was much deeper. He had to wade clumsily, with great physical effort. He was soon breathless. Then he stopped a moment, to steady himself again, and there was a sudden blast of wind out of the woods. It appeared to gather all the snow together, and fling it aside. Everything was snapped clear to him—the trees around, the house up ahead, the dark, dim glitter of a car over on the driveway, or else two cars. He had no chance to see what kind of cars they were, however. The snow swept back over him almost at once, and all he could see were those two lighted windows ahead of him on the first floor.

He stopped again. He was completely numbed by this time—feet, exposed face, even gloved hands. And he discovered that cold such as this did not cut like a knife at all. It had another effect. It gave Dillon the same sensation as the smash of a wooden club against him. There was the same stiffness and deadness of flesh, in the first instant before physical pain began to spread out from the point of impact, only this time the stiffness and deadness persisted instant after instant in him. He cursed breathlessly once more. How could he fire a rifle with numbed hands, and be sure of hitting what he aimed at? He could not, and there would of course be time for only one shot. Give it up, then? Wait for other and more favorable conditions tomorrow?

But that also seemed a contemptible shrinking away in him. He pushed on doggedly, and saw that the light was on between just two adjoining windows, so that apparently they were windows of the same room. The window over on his right had the shade drawn down to within an inch or two of the sill, but the shade over on his left was in the ordinary daytime position, only half drawn. So he was able to observe at least that part of the room, and to see an armchair, a fringed floor lamp with a yellow shade, an end table with a bottle of whiskey on it, and a drinking glass; then past the armchair a few pictures on a white plaster wall, and under the pictures a wooden bookcase with two encyclopedias on top, and beside them a blue and white China shepherdess holding her skirts daintily out to each side. It was quite obviously the Le Tendre living room, but the big armchair had no occupant at the moment. The tender one was not yet visible in there.

The whiskey bottle, however? The glass? Only these two windows lit in the whole building? Detective Dillon poked a small avalanche of snow from a low spreading pine branch in front of him with the rifle barrel, and then knelt. It seemed advisable to him to wait for a minute or two, and he did wait. Meanwhile he knocked more snow from the branch, and slid the end of the rifle over it.

But no good that way; not steady enough. He moved back—there was a slight upward slope at the edge of the lawn, so that he was almost on a direct level with anyone who would sit down in that armchair—and sprawled himself out in the approved sharpshooter's position. But then his feet were a little higher than his head, uncomfortably so; no good again. At last he discovered a firm, level area, and chose that. When he had settled himself, knees, toes, elbows, rifle, he put his head down against his left arm and attempted to rest for a moment; not to think.

But of course he did think; a scrap here, a scrap there. Rita; the dark brother; dead Chrissy; the clean hands business. Then finally he got hold of the one right thought with which to steady himself—Johnny, Johnny. He knew what he had to do after that, what he owed, at whatever cost to Detective Dillon personally; and so he again braced himself, dug his toes into the snow and raised his head.

The armchair was now occupied. Sitting there in full profile to him, as if obedient to the most explicit stage instructions from Detective Dillon himself, he saw Frenchy Le Tendre. He appeared to be talking to someone else in the room, and rather angrily. After a moment he leaned forward from the chair, wagging his forefinger, and then sitting back again with a sidewise but resentful shift of the whole body. After that he listened to someone, shaking his head two or three times, and keeping his lips firmly compressed. He appeared even angrier than before. He picked up a cigarette from the ashtray, inhaled deeply on it and then poured himself a drink from the whiskey bottle.

There was between them a distance of perhaps thirty feet, no more, which had to be considered practically unmissable range for Dillon the sharpshooter. He knew that. He assured himself of it, time after time. But who was in that room with Frenchy? He thought first that it was very likely the Palmer woman, but then a shadow was thrown over on the other window shade for Dillon. It was not the Palmer woman, after all. It was a man, and a big man; big as Vinson. But it was revealed only briefly to him, flickering from left to right on the shade, and then vanishing. He must have changed his place in the room. But he must also have been still talking, because Frenchy Le Tendre, half-smoked cigarette in his hand, whiskey glass poised halfway up to his mouth, was still listening.

At that point it was the dark brother who took over, and not John Patrick Dillon; no question about it. Because very carefully and deliberately, Dillon found, he had drawn a bead on Frenchy Le Tendre's left ear. What saved him there was that the tender one got up suddenly and abruptly, before Dillon the sharpshooter was quite ready, moved out of sight from the window and remained out of sight for at least a full minute. By that time John Patrick Dillon had gained himself a little breathing space, which he appeared to need badly. He was much better from then on; not a shake in him. At just the right instant he got the sense of purpose and dedication in him again, and knew that he was going to hit exactly what he wanted to hit. He stretched out flat in the snow, slipped the glove off his right hand and was all ready.

Frenchy came back. Frenchy lit another cigarette and sat down in the armchair. But he was not in quite so perfect a position now. He was leaning forward, hands between his knees, and so a little too close to the whiskey bottle. No good again. With only one shot to be offered, Detective Dillon wanted at least six clear inches between Le Tendre and that whiskey bottle; more, if possible. He waited for them.

Presently they came. Head up, looking at the other

person with a tough, cocky grin, Frenchy settled him-self a little more comfortably in the armchair, and crossed his legs. It was now perfect again. He was at least a foot and a half from the whiskey bottle. So Detective Dillon took in a long, even breath, according to manual, held it, and with a slow, steady pressure tightened his right forefinger.

The report came. It did not seem a very loud report to Dillon, certainly no louder than one of the trees cracking around him in this great cold, but just as it did come Frenchy Le Tendre leaned forward again to put his cigarette down, or started to, and at the same time there was a thick, dazzling swirl of loose snow out of the woods. Had the shot missed, then? Detective Dillon scrambled up, not sure yet, and heard the report flick-ing away from him like that snow along the ground, hearing and sight joined together for him in a rather odd manner. What had he hit, Frenchy or the whiskey bottle? He would have liked to be very sure about that, but he saw only the tender one flinging himself off side-ways at the report, or else being flung.

He went over in the other direction from Dillon, the big armchair following him, and he knocked the lamp down. It must have been the only lamp that had been turned on. Everything went pitch black now, Frenchy going over, the chair going over, the lamp going over. So there was only one thing for Detective Dillon to be sure of in all the desperate confusion he felt then; but the one thing was enough. He knew then that the dark brother had not missed, after all. There was just enough time, and enough light, for him to see the first outgush of blood, no mistake possible, from the exact center of Frenchy Le Tendre's left temple.

CHAPTER 5

When he saw that much, he began to run. But he had run no more than five or six steps in the heavy snow when he dropped the rifle, had to grope for it and then had to glare back over his shoulder at the Le Tendre house. It was not possible to see the window now, or even the house. So he ran desperately again, smashed head-on into the mailbox and then kept running.

But all the while he was trying to calm himself. No, he thought. He could never have missed a shot like that, not at the distance. Impossible for Dillon the sharpshooter; not to be thought of. Number One had been taken care of exactly as intended, and Number Two should be still sipping his brandy back in the hotel taproom. So he reached his car, threw his rifle into the back seat and dropped a blanket over it. And yet—had he missed? Could he have missed? It might have been a sliver of glass from the whiskey bottle that had hit Frenchy, and started the blood; but it might not. What in hell had happened back there? Couldn't he even remember now whether the whiskey bottle had been still whole and unmarked on the end table when he jumped up? If he had hit the whiskey bottle, then he had not hit Frenchy; and if he had hit Frenchy, then he had not hit the whiskey bottle. Which was the right answer for him?

He slued out onto the Forestville Road, stepping much too hard on the accelerator pedal, so that his back wheels gave a loud, angry whine, and then spun around uselessly, even with the new snow caps on. But he could not have missed, he again insisted; not Dillon the sharpshooter. And this time he did manage to convince himself; one down now, and one to go. He had successfully handled the first part of the thing. Now for the second.

He got the car under control, and headed straight back for Franklin Avenue. The dairy farm was still dark and quiet when he raced by, with no signs of commotion visible; but of course in this country, in this climate, everything would have been sealed up for the night hours ago. So who would have heard a single rifle report? He had fired only the one time. It had been all that was necessary for Dillon the sharpshooter.

He was not in panic any more about what he had hit; he had conquered that; but he was probably a bit nervous. He felt himself grin jumpily. There was no traffic on the Forestville Road this time, either, and none on Franklin Avenue, and when he turned left at the Town Hall he saw a police cruiser sitting placidly outside Rutherfurd's office, with no sudden activity boiling out from the side door. When he was past there, it seemed to him, he was past the one possible danger point, and with Number Two still unwarned and undefended against him. His schedule had worked out to the last second. He was way ahead.

But not the rifle this time, he warned himself; a lot too many people around in the Sachem Room. He would use the service revolver, after he had got Number Two out to the parking lot; much safer that way. So he turned right on Bridge Street, turned in at the rear entrance to the Harzard House and then parked his car as close as possible to the building itself.

Again he left his lights off and his motor on; a quick start for Detective Dillon from here, too. Frenchy Le Tendre had been the tricky and difficult part. Now he had only to walk straight ahead into the Sachem Room, approach the third wall booth from the street window and inquire of Number Two if he was the fellow that owned a gray Cadillac out in the parking lot. "Scraped your back fender," Number Two would be informed then. "Sorry. You want to come out and look at the damage, Jack?"

A very simple and natural excuse there, always the best kind. Number Two, a bit annoyed, perhaps, but with no warning yet about the Forestville Road, would unquestionably want to look at the damage; he would pick up his hat and coat; and Chris Dillon's brother, with no outward fuss or excitement in the Sachem Room, either, would walk out after him to the hotel parking lot. So it seemed to Dillon, when he pushed through the big glass doors into the hotel arcade, and turned right for the back passage to the Sachem Room, that the thing was as good as done already. It was just twenty-five minutes of one now. By a quarter past, without even the least hitch anywhere, he should be pulling into that nice, quiet double cabin of his over in North Falls.

The idea gave him a reckless impatience to get it all

finished now. Gripping the service revolver in his right overcoat pocket so that it would not sag down of its own weight in there, and perhaps be noticed by someone, he walked quickly ahead to the Sachem Room, and pushed open a swinging door from the back passage. That was when he discovered his first serious snag. The third wall booth from the street window was no longer occupied. Number Two, for whatever reason, had refused to wait obediently in position for him. What to do?

It seemed difficult to understand at first; not fair. He had set up everything in advance, detail by detail; yet now, with an empty booth facing him, his whole carefully arranged time schedule had become a pure shambles. He became aware that his right hand, still clamped around the service revolver in his overcoat pocket, had turned hot and slippery. And Number Two was not in the bar, he could see now; not in any other booth; not in the room. What had happened to him?

There was a group of men at the bar, all with two or three drinks before them, all very jovial. One of them stepped back into him, apologized for it and then blinked curiously when he saw Dillon's expression. At the moment it could not have been a normal expression. So this was how it was, Dillon was telling himself; this was why the people he had dealt with day after day persisted in making stupid and even incredible mistakes. They planned the whole thing in advance, as he had, and then a small matter of position or timing went wrong for them, and they began losing their heads. But of course Detective Dillon knew better than that, and much better. He would never lose his. Was Number Two still anywhere in the hotel? That was the first question. He moved over to the bar, and addressed the bartender.

"Where's Roy Vinson?" he demanded. "I had an

appointment in here with him at twelve-thirty. Where did he go?"

"Well, hang around a while," the bartender told him, also with a rather curious look; but it was a pale and tense Detective Dillon who was reflected now in the bar mirror, and so no wonder about that. "He was here just a little while ago. Talking to a girl, I think. Maybe he went out to the lobby with her."

A girl? Dillon asked himself. But why not? That would be altogether in character for Number Two. So he went out hurriedly into the back passage, inspected the men's washroom there and then trotted around to the main lobby. He was losing time now; very precious time. The panic seemed to be edging back.

It was a big, cavernous lobby. At one end was the desk, and at the other end a small bandstand had been set up, and the chairs and couches moved clear. The bandstand had been covered with pink crepe, and trailers of colored paper had been festooned around under the ceiling. "Looks kind of nice, don't it?" the old elevator man asked him. "They're fixing it up for the Winter Carnival Ball next weekend. You going up, mister?"

"No, thanks," Dillon managed for him. "Not just yet." But the car, he thought then; the gray Cadillac. If that was still here, then so was Number Two. Again he hurried out through the arcade passage, trying not to hurry too much with the elevator man still watching him, and found the car, or a gray Cadillac, at any rate, over at the far end of the parking lot. Was it the right car, however? That became another distracting uncertainty for him. Roy Vinson's Cadillac, in his one glimpse of it earlier this evening over in front of 147 Lake Avenue, had appeared to him a darker, shinier gray, and the real big Cadillac model, not this type. But was he sure about that?

He discovered that he was not sure of anything at all at the moment. He moved over to his own car, turned off the ignition switch and took his keys out. Where was Number Two? Could he have gone upstairs with that girl of his for a little privacy? Then which room? The elevator man, he thought then, and trotted desperately back into the hotel again. But he had no luck there, either. Yes, the elevator man did know Mr. Roy Vinson; but no, the elevator man had not taken him upstairs at any time tonight.

It seemed to be a complete dead end. And what time was it now? The lobby clock showed Dillon. It was ten minutes of one, and more precious time slipping away. He tried the bar again; no luck. He went out to Main Street, checked the cars parked in front of the hotel and checked Dewdrop's Tavern. When he got back to the Sachem Room, the Town Hall clock had just struck a single ponderous note, and they were turning the juke box off, and the window lights.

"Sorry," the bartender told him; the same bartender. "I can't serve you, mister. We're just closing up."

"But I tell you I was supposed to meet Roy Vinson," he insisted stupidly. "Where did he go?"

"Well, you can hang around," the bartender said, "till these people here finish their drinks. I don't know where he went, mister. I can't tell you."

Hang around, Dillon thought, and with that fine lead of his ticking away second by second now. Yet what else offered itself? If he tried 147 Lake Avenue, he might miss Number Two coming back here. Better stay. He moved over to the bar, so that he could watch the back door and the front door, and the two bartenders began cleaning up, and checking the cash register. Then at ten minutes past one, after throwing his towel down at the far end of the bar, the stout, bald-headed bartender came around to lock the street door.

By that time there were only four or five people in the whole place.

"Come on," the bartender urged them. "Drink up now. Give us a break, will you? I got to lock up."

Then the door to the back passage was thrown open, but it was not Number Two who came in from that direction. It was Charley Dooley. He wore an old woodsman's cap and a red Mackinaw, and with most of the lights off he had no chance to recognize Dillon standing against the bar. Perhaps he would not have recognized him in any event. He looked very excited about something.

"Hey, fellows!" he said. "You hear yet what happened to Frenchy Le Tendre tonight? He got the whole goddam top of his head blown off. Where's Rutherfurd? Jerry Brenner's out in the lobby looking for him. They think it's Art Palmer."

Somebody else bustled in after him, a stout, red-faced town patrolman, obviously Jerry Brenner, and the same man Dillon remembered from last summer in Rutherfurd's office. There was a lot of commotion for everybody in the Sachem Room then, or for almost everybody. It was only John Patrick Dillon, elbows still on the bar, head down, who remained silent and motionless for at least a full minute. He felt nothing but a sickeningly dull lassitude of thought and physical action. One phrase kept repeating itself over and over in his mind—the whole goddam top of his head blown off.

Then he manged to straighten himself somewhat. But of course, he told himself. Dillon the sharpshooter might be a very fine marksman, indeed; but what he understood now was that his dark brother, at the one critical instant tonight, had proved himself to be a much better one. He knew now what he had hit; not the whiskey bottle. Yet he had refused to believe it until this moment. It was like Chris all over again. He had not been able to face up to the plain fact. Still standing against the bar, eyes down, hands back again in his overcoat pockets, he managed to glance in a heavily fixed manner from the patrolman to Charley Dooley.

"And I tell you a sweeter guy never lived," Poor Old Charley was declaring shrilly and emotionally now to the whole room, actual tears in his eyes. "We went down to the World's Fair together a couple of years ago. We did everything together. I tell you it was that lousy little bastard Art Palmer. He was threatening Frenchy over in the Red Dog the other night, when he had his load on. I heard him myself. But I never thought—"

Then he saw Dillon standing against the bar, and recognized him. And of course, Detective Dillon found himself reflecting quite calmly, Poor Old Charley had seen his rifle this afternoon. Would he make the connection? But he made it instantly, with that unerring craftiness of his. At once his expression changed. He got a weak, nervous grin on his lips, and tried to shelter himself back of the nearest bartender.

"Well, hi there," he began babbling. "I see you stayed over, buddy. I see—"

Then Dillon began to move; had to. He did not want to hurt anybody here in the Sachem Room, and it seemed to him that the only thing he had left now was that his act against Frenchy Le Tendre must be considered a simple and justified act. So he wanted to keep it like that, and when he found himself able to move at last he managed everything with sudden and even brutal quickness. He knew how important the first few seconds always were. He tried to use them.

The first thing he did was to shove the bartender out of his way, and over against Jerry Brenner. Then he got hold of Dooley by the front of the Mackinaw, with his left hand, and began to back off toward the rear passage step by step, with Dooley beginning to squirm and then squeal frantically against him. He did not even realize that he had the service revolver in his right hand until one of the waitresses screamed, and the remaining bartender ducked down into a booth hurriedly.

But he had reached the door by that time. He kicked it open behind him, and then flung Dooley head-on at the other bartender. After that there was a great deal of confusion. Poor Old Charley caught at a couple of the bar stools to save himself; they went over on top of him; and the two bartenders began shouting.

Which was the way it began for John Patrick Dillon, one department gold medal, five citations for meritorious police conduct. He had promised himself not to run afterward; but he did run. He had the idea that he was fully and finally integrated now with the dark brother; no choice about that, either, and so he had only enough time to understand that he had finished just half of the job so far, the less important half, and that Number Two still waited for him. It was no good to turn back now, after Frenchy Le Tendre. What could he turn back to? He had to go on. So the moment he was clear of everyone in the back hall he jammed up the exit behind him by knocking a wooden bench across it, and then ripped a bulky coat rack from against the wall, and added that. It might have gained him a few seconds. He was out in the parking lot, at any rate, before anyone at all could get through the door behind him.

But there was one more complication waiting for him out there. He realized immediately, or the dark brother did, that his own car was out of service for him from now on. He would have to jump in, start the motor again, and in this weather, but even then he would not be able to get out of the parking lot. There was a police cruiser blocking the driveway now, red roof light flashing around, motor humming. The door to it, on the driver's side, was still hanging wide open the way Jerry Brenner must have left it minutes ago.

And the dark brother understood at once what to do about that; not an instant of hesitation. He used the police cruiser. He smashed it into reverse, whined back to Bridge Street, smashed it around out there after again skidding dangerously, and then got himself straightened out for the North Falls Road that lay directly ahead.

But even the dark brother realized now the one fatal mistake he had made. He should have started with Number Two! Why hadn't he? Yet it might be still possible to finish with him. He had some kind of a start now, and he had to improve it. When he roared away from the Hazard House there was no one out yet in the parking lot, and along Bridge Street there were only a few parked cars, and no pedestrians. There was, however, a stop sign two blocks ahead, where Bridge Street led in at a sharp angle to the state highway. But the police cruiser did not slow up for that stop sign. It put on speed, rather. There was, thankfully, no traffic coming along in either direction.

But once out on the state highway it came to Dillon that he no longer had a secure sanctuary waiting for him in North Falls. Perhaps he would be able to cover the eighteen or twenty miles back there before Frank Rutherfurd could call ahead and get the road blocks set up; but in the event that he did make it, the police cruiser could be identified at sight by even a small boy, wherever it was abandoned finally. Let it be abandoned in North Falls, and the search for John Patrick Dillon would be immediately concentrated in that area, and not here. He had put a millstone around his neck with this car, wherever he took it. Unless . . .

The last village street light dropped behind him, standing high and lonely for a moment in thick snow. Unless what? A solid white world dropped in around him, broken only by the low yellow glare of his headlights rushing along the road. Unless, he decided hurriedly, he could think of a way to make the police cruiser vanish somehow or other into thin air. Then there might be a very faint chance for him with Number Two. If the cruiser could not be found anywhere at all either tonight or tomorrow, Rutherfurd would have to assume that he had broken through for the Canadian border, or south for Albany. Then he might be able to finish off the rest of his simple and justified act—if he kept them puzzled and uncertain as to his whereabouts, if he kept them dispersed, if they had to hunt to hell and gone all over this central Adirondack area in weather like this for Dillon the murderer, and if all the time he was still here in Hazard Lake waiting his chance at Number Two.

If, if, if! Yet without the police cruiser to show where he was, they would have to believe that he had slipped free on one of the back roads over to Tupper Lake, or perhaps north to Malone. But how to dispose of the cruiser? That was the essential problem here, and he had very little time in which to solve it. So what kind of perfect hiding place offered itself to him along this North Falls Road? Just ahead, he knew, lay Dooley's gas station, with the Catholic school on the hill opposite, then a few hamburger and souvenir stands, the auto graveyard, Jack Riley's snack bar, and one or two dingy motels. He could hide the cruiser off in the woods, and Rutherfurd would find it. He could hide it behind one of the hamburger stands, and Rutherfurd would find it there, too. But there was one place, it flashed on him, where Rutherfurd would never find it, not until hell froze over—and the dark brother made an instant and unerring decision about that place.

He roared past the Catholic school, and past Dooley's. A little beyond there he turned off to the right, very careful to leave no wide skid marks behind him, and began bumping ahead over an open field. When he had got in about a hundred yards from the road, he turned left, drove another few feet, drove around to face back to the road again and got out of the car.

He worked with a kind of savage rapidity after that, in fierce, freezing Adirondack cold again, and in pitch blackness. He used the flashlight to open the cruiser trunk, to get out the jack lever and the jack base, and then to set the pointed end of the lever against the roof police emblem. After that, working in full dark again, he was able to punch through a small hole under the emblem, and then by prying up with the jack, rip the emblem clean off.

He had just finished with that part when he heard a siren whining out toward him from back in the village. He crouched down, but the faint headlight glow on the road raced by without even slowing down for a moment, and he was able to set to work again. This time he used the jack lever to club down the few upturned edges of metal on the roof, to smash the windshield and to pry at one of the back doors until it hung down and aside crookedly by one hinge. That satisfied him. The jack lever he threw back into the trunk, then the jack base and after that the roof signal light.

Two other cars, moving at much more moderate speeds, went past over on the state highway. Then he could see an old Roadmaster Buick, circa 1949, to his left, and on the other side a ruined pickup truck. Pretty good, Dillon told himself. He had judged his location all right. He had the police cruiser sitting in just about the geographical center of the Hazard Lake auto graveyard, and Poor Old Charley had told him that twelve inches of snow was expected by tomorrow morning. So by daylight every car on the field would have a thick, level coating of snow over it, and without the roof emblem, in the middle of a couple of hundred other wrecked vehicles, there seemed a very good chance to him that the police cruiser would never be discovered or even suspected in here until next spring.

Which solved his first problem. Now let Rutherfurd find out what had happened to it, and to Dillon—if Rutherfurd could. They had made their first mistake by rushing to block off the North Falls Road against him. They would probably make others. But they could afford to make them, and one after another. Dillon could not. And now he was confronted by a second and even more urgent necessity—lodging for the night. Where could he find it?

That was an even tougher question for him. He understood that he must be fully identified by this time, or would be in the next half hour or so. Poor Old Charley would certainly blab out his story about the rifle, first of all; then the bartender would put in that the same fellow in the sheepskin coat had been inquiring all night for Roy Vinson; and between Number One and Number Two Frank Rutherfurd could not miss the one inevitable conclusion. Every necessary detail would be known and at once broadcast about him—his name, his physical description, the way he was dressed.

And therefore every place of public accommodation in and around Hazard Lake was off limits for him. He had no car any longer, and no baggage. He would be recognized immediately; Rutherfurd would be informed immediately; and yet he had to find livable shelter for himself in this weather. It might drop to thirty or thirty-five below in the predawn hours; it did, up in the central Adirondacks during these months. Eddie McManus had told him, and Eddie had been born and brought up over in Lake Placid. You couldn't even sit down under a tree for half an hour to rest yourself, because if you did the cold made you feel drowsy and light-headed; you dropped off to sleep pretty quick; and then they found you next morning frozen stiff as a board. He was hungry and tired now. He would get much more so if he attempted to keep moving around all night. For supper he should have had something substantial and nourishing, instead of that damned fish. Why hadn't he? Of course, though. Friday.

Friday. . . . All at once he saw the importance of that day of the week for him. He saw where the right kind of private and comfortable shelter was waiting for him, and not very far off, either. So he got out the flashlight again, grinning nervously, snapped it off and on in brief spurts and very soon found his way back to the state highway.

His shelter was only about a half a mile back toward the village. Twice during that distance he had to shelter himself in the woods when he heard a car coming, but each time he trotted on again, and then at last saw Dooley's gas station ahead of him, one dim light on down in the office, but none at all in the apartment upstairs.

He slipped over to the other side of the road at that point, deciding to circle in toward the back of his sanctuary from the woods. He would leave no footprints visible from the road then; much safer—or he would leave none moving straight up to the front door, at any rate. Yet he found at once that even this close to town there were very thick woods, and made for very difficult going. In the darkness he could hear only a light, crisp rustling under the trees, and see nothing. Sleet, he told himself. Now the footing would become treacherous. Had he come in too far, and missed his way?

There was no option but to use the flashlight once more, despite the risk. It showed him ghostly dark trees, and the heavy snow coming down around him in great, pouring swirls, always whipping faster and faster at him, and yet always suspended miraculously in black air. He became a little frightened then—the darkness, the great cold, the almost perfect quiet—and remembered another story that Eddie McManus had told him.

That one concerned a hunter who had got lost out in the woods during hunting season. So that night, according to Eddie, a lot of people had gone out looking for him with big yellow lanterns. They found him, too, but every time he saw the lanterns around he began to howl like a mad dog, and to run away from them, not toward them. In the end they all had to spread out in a long line, and run him down. He kept screaming and screaming the whole time, and yet he had only been lost for about four hours. "But you have no idea what kind of country it is," Eddie told him. "Pretty rugged, John. It just scares the living hell out of you to be left alone in it, that's all. You wouldn't believe it, would you?"

Now Dillon believed it. There were no more spurts and blusters of wind, but a steady and almost soundless rushing on over the trees, like a distant express train that hummed by endlessly. Invisible tree branches whipped back at him after he turned off the flashlight, and ripped the left side of his sheepskin coat. Then he fell over a rock, and twisted his left knee painfully.

It was no use that way; the flashlight again. A dim white tunnel spun out under the snow for him, and at last, off to the side, showed him the blessed vision of two wooden uprights with a long cross bar between them. He was oriented then. He waded out of the woods, waded around one end of the football goal-posts and approached his sanctuary.

Almost a solid row of windows faced him, all on the one floor. There was an ash barrel by the back door, and a legend on it in white paint that advised PROP-ERTY OF SAINT JOSEPH'S SCHOOL. DO NOT REMOVE! Then it seemed to him that he was in good order once more, with at least some kind of chance at those two clear days for himself. It was indeed Friday night, and so there would be no school here tomorrow, and none Sunday. But how to get in?

That was the next problem; coming one after another now. If he smashed one of the windows, or forced the back door, he would leave very evident traces behind himself, and the first trooper who came around inves-tigating St. Joseph's would realize what had happened. No good that way. Rutherfurd was a cop, too; and rule one in the rookies' handbook, when anything like this happened, was to check the neighborhood, check it again and keep checking until the fugitive had been captured or identified somewhere else.

Was there a key, then? He could see inside to the hall. The upper part of the door was clear glass, and not two inches away, but around on the other side of the world for him, there was a key, all right. It was clearly visible. At midpoint along the hall, which appeared to run from front to back of the building, there was a blue night light plugged in low down on the wall, just over a brown baseboard. It showed him a dim entry up front, a few dark, open doorways on each side and a linoleum floor.

But the key. At one time Detective Dillon had spent almost a year on the Burglary Squad, and he remembered now that it was sometimes possible to slip a piece of paper under the door, to poke out the key from the other side with a pocket nailfile, and then to withdraw paper and key for oneself by pulling gently. It was not, however, possible here at St. Joseph's. The door had been fitted neatly and tightly along the bottom, with no room for even a small key to be drawn under, and this was a big, solid one, with a thick handle.

The lock itself, then? No. It was a simple and uncomplicated bolt lock, just a square metal box under the knob, and so altogether foolproof. A snap lock he could have managed by working patiently with a bit of cellophane, perhaps one of the card slips from his wallet case; but a bolt lock, where a solid metal shaft slid over tight as a drum into the wall opening, gave him no opportunity of that kind. Then the roof? There would have to be a skylight up there, perhaps a door. Could he scramble up to the roof?

But at the last moment he saw another and much better possibility here. The back door opened out from the school hall, which he remembered vaguely was a law now for all places of public assemblage, not in. Both the hinges were on his side of the door, consequently one of them high up near the top, and the other one low down near the bottom.

Then it ought to be simple enough, Dillon told himself. All he had to do was slip the bolts out, and then he could ease the hinged end of the door little by little from the wall connections. He set to work. He got a dime from his pocket, and tried that, attempting to insert the dime between the bolt head and the top of the hinge, but the dime proved useless to him. It slipped off. It slipped off a second time. He tried foolishly to hammer it under the bolt head with his palm, and it rebounded into the snow behind him, with the bolt solid as rock yet. After that he had to put his gloves back on, and keep his hands under his armpits in order to warm them up briefly. The sleet whispered and pattered. The express train over the trees rushed on minute after minute. There was now a glaze of thick, frozen snow on his shoulders, down the whole front of his sheepskin coat and on his gloves.

Something sharp, he told himself; something pointed. The spike on his belt buckle? He let his belt dangle down, got the tip of his belt buckle under the bolt hole and tapped up against it with a small rock. But that was the top bolt; the easy bolt. The bottom one was another proposition for him.

To manage that, first of all, he had to lay himself out flat on the stone entry. Even then he could only manage the business in cramped, awkward fashion. He could no longer hammer up with enough force, considering the distance available to him, to get the bolt started, and he had to try it the other way after a time, trying to slip in the point of the spike between the hinge and the bolt head. He had to try and try. Finally he succeeded, however.

Then it was required to rest a minute or so; pretty well spent. But at least the worst part of the job was now over. Once he had drawn out the two bolts, he could work the top hinge a little away from the wall connection, and then the bottom hinge. Time after time he did that; very patient—top hinge, bottom hinge. The last part was the worst. He did not want to leave any scrapes or dents on the side of the door frame, and yet when he had the door hanging almost completely free to him it jammed up. He set his teeth, tried again and heard a sharp, ominous creak from the lock side, as if the bolt over there was now being forced out of position against the slot. But he was very patient again—top hinge, bottom hinge. At last he managed it.

Yet in managing it he almost ruined the whole business. When he had the door free and clear, he was stupid enough to set it against the wall of the building, and it toppled out suddenly, from a blast of wind whipping behind it. He had to throw his body in front at the last moment, and catch the door in both arms against himself. In that way he was able to prevent the glass pane from smashing down in a thousand pieces on the floor of the entry; but he wrenched his left knee even more painfully this time. At last he pushed himself up, still holding the door, staggered around like a drunken man and slipped the two door hinges back into the two sets of interlocking wall loops. After that he had only to pat the bolts down, to go on into the hall, to unlock the door with the key which was now available to him and then to lock it again.

There was a low radiator in the hall. He sat down there, shaking a bit, and discovered that two of his fingertips and his right palm had been scraped raw. Blood on the door, too? He checked it carefully with the flashlight, inside and out, then used his handkerchief to remove the few spots of blood that he found, and a couple of dirt stains. After that he could see no marks on the door, or on the wall of the building. He sat down on the radiator again, feeling more shaky now that all the immediate cause for tension was over with, and remained sitting for about five minutes. There was just a little heat on in the radiator; night heat. He let it penetrate. Then, the most bitterly freezing numbness having worn off, he stood up again, and brushed the snow from his coat.

Toward the front of the building he found a small storage closet; mops and buckets. He cleaned up all the snow that had drifted in when he had the door open, and used his flashlight in one of the classrooms. It must have been the first grade classroom; twenty or thirty small desks, a big one up front for the teacher, and a row of colored animals pasted up over the windows. I have a dog, Dillon read from oversized and effortfully angular writing on the blackboard. Ned is my dog. I like Ned. On the same side of the corridor as the storage closet was a coatroom, with two or three rows of hooks shining emptily, and the principal's office.

He returned to the back door, peered out at the snow that was still falling, perhaps falling heavier than before, indeed, and saw a faint reflection of Dillon the murderer facing him. Dillon the murderer. . . . But it was still difficult to accept that. There was a correction to be made, Dillon felt; and yet what correction? Who had driven out to the Forestville Road a few hours ago? Who had fired his one shot carefully and deliberately from the approved sharpshooter's position? But he could explain all that to Frank Rutherfurd, of course; not John Patrick Dillon at all, but the dark brother.

And yet no matter which of them had fired the shot, the issue here had become a matter of simple personal survival by this time. The old values were all gone. The old rules of conduct had to be considered as entirely changed over for him. Dillon the murderer . . .

For perhaps five minutes he stood there looking out at the snow, and tried to think of it not as an enemy any more, but a friend, rather. Soon now his footprints would be covered up outside, every one of them; nothing for Rutherfurd. And back in the auto graveyard snow would be piling up inch after inch on the wrecked police cruiser; nothing there, either. He had managed the first part of the thing, and there was obviously nothing to do now but decide how he could finish it with Number Two. That was the important half. That had to be done yet. It had to be done more than ever, indeed, after Frenchy Le Tendre.

Very probably he would be able to think of something in due time. Now, at any rate, he had the whole weekend to think about it—unless one of the nuns showed up here. Was that likely? Only the event itself could prove that to him, he decided finally, but it was certain that no teaching sister would come over here from the convent in this storm, and at this hour of night. He was safe enough for the moment, consequently. Something to eat, then? He investigated the other parts of the building.

In front there was another and much longer hall, and a couple more night lights, one set halfway along in each wing. Turn them off? He decided against that. The best thing would be to have St. Joseph's appear normal in every respect if anyone came around to investigate it before daylight, and of course he would have warning enough to get out of sight if they did that, because he would hear their car grinding up to the front door, or see their headlights. But a quick outside check ought to satisfy them for tonight, anyway. As Detective Dillon would have done in similar circumstances, they would only look over the windows from outside, the front door and the back door. And what would they find? Everything in serene order; not a hint of forced entry at any point. So they would give it up, and go on to try their luck at other places; and by daylight tomorrow morning, with their police cruiser still missing, it would have to be considered that Dillon the murderer was a couple of hundred miles off now, and still going. The something to eat, however?

At the far end of the building he found a combined gymnasium and lunchroom. But there must have been a basketball game this afternoon, because the chairs and tables had all been pushed back to one wall.

There were tall, wide windows on three sides, with wire mesh covering them, and on the fourth side a long counter of stainless steel. Beyond that was the kitchen; a dim glitter of pots and pans on the wall, an oversized work table, a big electric range with a hood over it and two double-doored automatic refrigerators.

All the comforts of home, Dillon thought. Food, shelter, warmth—but of course every school in the country served daily lunches to their student body in these times. The dark brother had made another unerring selection for him in St. Joseph's. And he was very hungry by now, or very empty, it might be. But somewhere he had read that ravenous hunger was the invariable reaction after killing a man. Probably the old caveman instinct; first the hunt, then the belly filled. Dillon the murderer . . .

He attempted to stop thinking about that part. He cooked two hot dogs for himself, opened up a can of spaghetti and heated enough water for two cups of instant coffee. Then while waiting he took a small sip of brandy from his pocket flask, and had a cigarette. Then he washed the dishes and utensils he had used, replaced them and limped back to the principal's office.

It would be about his best observation point during the night. By leaving one door open, the one out to the front hall, he could watch the entry vestibule while invisible and unsuspected himself in the dark office; and by leaving the other door open, the one out to the side hall, he could slip off in that direction if and when it seemed advisable to him. So he put an armchair in position, pulled over a second one for his legs and settled down. The service revolver was still in his right overcoat pocket, and he still had his hand on it; the old standby for him now. Of course. Dillon the murderer . . .

Cold fact now; proven fact. So why fight it any more?

He had decided what he was going to do, Dillon re-membered, even while he was still talking to Ruther-furd last night; Number One for him, and then Number Two. But after that he had been very cunning about tricking himself. He had pretended that he could do the thing for Chris in another way, a right way, but the chances were that he had never truly believed that at all. It had only been the dark brother craftily leading on John Patrick Dillon to what he had done against Frenchy Le Tendre. So now he had to go on with it, with Number Two still waiting for him. To turn back at this point, and to protest hypocritically that it had been some kind of accident, and that he had never intended to kill Frenchy at all, would be contemptible and shame-less in him. The only possible thing to do was to go on, and complete the thing; but what were his chances and possibilities now in regard to Number Two? He would have to start thinking about that.

First, then, Frank Rutherfurd was now fully alerted. He might set up a police guard day and night at 147 Lake Avenue until Dillon the murderer had been found; he might keep Number Two at some secret hideaway in Hazard Lake, although still under police protection; and he might, the really foolproof method, slip Number Two out of town for the next couple of days until Dillon the murderer had been found.

In any case it would be necessary to keep running a lot longer than Dillon had intended to run. There would be much time and thought needed to complete the arrangements for Number Two. That neat, tight schedule of his had spun altogether out of control back in the Sachem Room a few hours ago. And an-other thing. Dillon the murderer had even yanked out his service revolver back there. For what reason? He could not possibly have used it on Number Two. Num-ber Two was not present. On whom, then? On one of

John Patrick Dillon's own kind, even on Frank Ruther-furd, perhaps, if Rutherfurd had been around? He was progressing, all right; learning fast. And Rita had warned him the other night. Whatever he might do to Roy Vinson, Rita had said, whatever might satisfy him, he would be doing something much worse to himself. She had been right, too. He was beginning to see it at last. Dillon the murderer . . .

Suddenly he got up, not to think about Rita any more, and discovered that there was a noticeable swelling and tenderness around his left knee; more pain, also. Another nice little touch. He no longer had trans-portation available; his identity and description must be known to everybody in Hazard Lake by this time; and now the damned knee was beginning to act up. So why was he still thinking of Number Two? Was he out of his mind?

He began to prowl restlessly; back door, front door. The school electric clock showed him that it was twenty minutes past two, and a framed photograph of old Pope John regarded him with a wide, beaming smile over one of the night lights. It was still snowing, and at twenty-five minutes of three they came around with the first snow plow. He heard a metallic grinding and clanking down on the road, and presently could watch a big truck pushing along, and two workmen, both heavily muffled, dumping out shovels of sand over the backboard.

But that was a brief interlude. Soon the snow plow was out of sight, having permitted him to glimpse a world where neither earth nor sky could be seen, noth-ing but a small patch of the road and the snow coming down over it, and then the red taillights receding little by little from him past Dooley's gas station. Again, while watching the truck, he found that he had slipped the service revolver into his right hand, and again he could not even remember taking it from his overcoat pocket. The simple and justified act . . .

He hobbled back to the school kitchen, found a long wooden bench in there and lay down. He did not intend to sleep; he was very tired, it seemed to him, but not sleepy at all; and yet he got the idea presently that he was out in the woods back of St. Joseph's. This time a profound stillness reigned. He could see vague dark trees, the snow falling silently and one yellow lantern directly ahead of him.

He seemed to be running and running for that lantern, and shouting at it. Then all at once he could see that it wasn't a lantern at all, but a lighted window, and he could remember the window. So he threw up both of his arms before him, not to see anything that happened in there, and was confronted out of the dark by the dead, cold face of Frenchy Le Tendre. He turned in the other direction, crazy panic in him, and was confronted by the dead, cold face of Christina Elizabeth Dillon. He ran. One on each side, never more than a foot distant from Dillon the murderer, they succeeded in keeping effortless pace with him.

It was not any too warm in the school kitchen. Yet he found thick sweat on him when he woke up, and he began to curse breathlessly. He had another drink of the brandy, and made another round of the building. It was still pitch black outside, not a glimmer of dawn visible, and still snowing. The wind, a bit quieter than before, but never still, made a monotonous low whine around every corner of the school building.

He decided not to listen to it, but to other things. He began hearing the other things. He heard his own footsteps, scuffling a bit because of his bad knee, but then it seemed to him that he heard other and more furtive steps back in the corridor. He stopped instantly; jaws clamped, service revolver all ready, and attempted to make sure of the other steps in that fashion. They stopped. He went on again. At once, at the same second of time, so did they.

In the kitchen he made more coffee and ate the rest of the spaghetti, not bothering to clean up this time. But after that it seemed a good idea to him that every half hour from now on, just in case, he make another inspection tour, and he did that at half past four, and at five o'clock. Nothing had changed either time. He went back to the bench, lay down wearily on it, just to rest his bad knee for a while and then dozed off once more. The next time he opened his eyes it was full daylight.

CHAPTER *6*

Then winter sunlight streamed in cheerfully over him through the kitchen windows, and he could see the athletic field outside, with not even a single animal mark showing itself yet on the fresh snow. Everything glittered. Overhead was a dazzling January sky, all pure, tender blue, and far off in the aseptically clean and cold mountain air he could pick out the ascending series of uprights that marked off the public ski lift over toward North Falls, miles and miles distant. The knee ached dully, and so did his right arm, where he had been lying on it. The time was ten minutes past eight Saturday morning.

He sat up on the bench. The moment he did that, although he still heard nothing out in the hall, or in any other part of the building, he was at once positive that there was someone here in St. Joseph's with him. But before he could do anything at all about that, he saw the door to the hall being pushed open, and the nun come in. She seemed to Dillon a very old nun, and a very undersized one, perhaps up to his shoulder. She had a thin gray face, darker gray eyelids, and a brisk, almost dainty manner. She appeared to be talking to herself. There was no one with her.

"Now, really," Dillon heard, while she was still closing the door after herself. "The day hardly begun so far, and yet distraction at Mass twice, and a vile, mean outburst of temper about that horrible coffee at breakfast. Oh, sister, sister! Can't you ever understand that you make me despair sometimes? Nothing but pamper and pet for you, with this fault to be excused, naturally, and that one glossed over. When even the simplest examination of conscience—"

Then she started ahead for the work table, and saw Dillon, who felt himself sharply alert in mind against her, but at the same time stupidly numbed in physical action. At once she elevated the thin old brows imperiously, while remaining calm and severe in facial expression. There was a sheet of paper in her right hand, and when she had moved on to the other side of the work table, again with that rather impressive physical daintiness of hers, she began tapping the paper against her black skirt time after time.

"But my dear man!" she began then, in a completely assured and authoritative manner. "My dear man! Now I must say! You will please stand up over there, and remove your cap. What is the meaning of this? Who are you, sir? And how did you ever manage to get yourself here into St. Joseph's at this hour?"

But those were all questions that had no meaning for Dillon. There was another, much more urgent. Was she alone? He got up hurriedly, moved around the other side of the work table from her and opened the door.

The morning sun, by reflection, made it as pleasant and bright out in the front hall as in the kitchen. He limped forward into the hall, making no attempt to answer her. He was not yet in sufficient control of himself to think of an answer.

She had followed him.

"But my dear man!" she repeated, even more imperiously. "Just one moment now. I merely happen to be the principal of this school, Sister Mary Frances, and I believe you would be well advised to answer my questions. What do you want in this building? How in the world did you get in last night? What is your business?"

He understood how he must look to her. There was the old sheepskin coat, torn in front, and badly rust-stained from his exertions last night in the auto grave-yard; the further fact that he had been given no chance to shave or wash this morning; and of course the expression, which he himself felt, of an ugly and yet uncontrollable dark glitter of the eyes toward her. So he remained silent. Already he had noticed a battered old Jeep standing outside by the front door, and the two sets of footprints leading from it. One undoubtedly belonged to Sister Mary Frances. They were narrow and pointed. The other, judging by their size and depth in the snow, would have to be masculine. Who was with her?

He had little time to consider the problem. Glancing out at the Jeep from one of the hall windows, he also found himself glancing out at Dooley's gas station on the other side of the state highway, and at the two men who were talking over there by one of the pumps. The first man wore the uniform of a state trooper. The second, tall and gaunt as ever in a dark overcoat and gray cap, was Frank Rutherfurd.

At once he drew himself away from the window,

twisting the knee before he thought, and then wincing painfully. Sister Mary Frances gave him a sharp, steady look, moved over to the place he had just vacated and saw the same two men presented to her. Then she folded her hands high and primly under that oblong white chest piece they all wore, nodded her head and considered Dillon from tip to toe once more.

"So that's it," she said. "I see. You even have the police after you. Then what did you attempt to do around here last night? Were you trying to break into Mr. Dooley's gas station for yourself, before breaking in here? Is that it? Are you a thief, sir?"

He stood back against the wall, still facing her. But Dillon the thief, it came to him, would be a much better interpretation for her than Dillon the murderer. Quite obviously she had not heard yet. Teaching nuns went to bed early; they got up early, for six or seven o'clock Mass every morning; and they lived secluded to themselves in a school convent. So what promised here if she did not know anything at all about Frenchy Le Tendre, and if he could manage her in the right way? It was a very small hope with Rutherfurd and the state trooper within call opposite, but it was the only hope. He tried, therefore, to look and act properly hangdog about himself.

"I don't know anything about that gas station," he declared surlily. "You oughtn't to say such things, sister. Look around in here, if you want to. Go ahead. What could I take?"

"Now, now." The chin came up; a severe forefinger cautioned him to better manners with her. "None of that, sir. No impudent defiance, thank you. You made coffee for yourself out in my kitchen, and ate something. I saw the dish."

He risked another look over at the gas station. Now, hands behind him, head shaking slowly and rather gloomily, Rutherfurd was walking on into the office. The state trooper went in after him. But for how long? It was probable that they intended to check the whole neighborhood out here, which meant that Dillon needed all the time he could get, and all the help, too. What time and what help could Sister Mary Frances be induced to give him? He made himself drop his eyes in a shamefaced and reluctant manner, not to look at her; the detected thief's natural attitude.

"All right," he said. "I'll tell you the truth, sister. A guy hit me in Dewdrop's Tavern last night, and I hit him back. Then they called for the cops. All I wanted was some kind of a place to sleep it off. Give me a break, can't you? They'd hand me ninety days for something like this. I only cooked a couple of hot dogs for myself, and made some coffee. What did I hurt?"

"Now that," Sister Mary Frances declared stonily, and yet with a slightly fluttery gesture of the clasped hands, as if a little helpless or uncertain now, "that I intend to find out in a very few minutes, sir. Don't you worry at all. Did you break a lock last night, or one of the windows? How did you get in here?"

He decided on a weak, shamed grin.

"Didn't have to," he mumbled. "The back door wasn't locked. I tried the gas station first, but some guy began hollering at me from upstairs. I didn't know what to do. I've only got about thirty cents in my pocket."

"All over the bar," she said, nodding the old head grimly. "Of course; fighting and drinking. And now we're very proud of ourselves this morning, aren't we? I suppose this is a regular Friday night occurrence for you, week after week?"

"First time," he mumbled again, "that I touched a drop since last summer. Honest to God, sister. I took the pledge."

"And I can see kept it," she declared witheringly. "Well, don't bother to swear anything else to me, sir. Save your breath. So you're a Catholic, are you?"

He made a pathetic gesture of concession with his left hand, still trying to look over at Dooley's gas station. But he understood the road now for Sister Mary Frances. All the miserably offered excuses to Detective Dillon in the old days came back to him—the excuses of weakness, of bad company, but good intentions; of what had been meant, rather than what had been done, actually.

"And I can see a very devout one," Sister Mary Frances said, still eyeing him with no favor. "Breaking the pledge; drinking yourself silly and quarrelsome in Dewdrop's Tavern; and then, to cap everything else, having the barefaced audacity to walk right in here, here to St. Joseph's, and to cook two hot dogs for yourself on Friday night. Well, that's fine, sir. That's a really splendid performance. What next, I wonder?"

It was getting a bit humorous to Dillon now; sardonically twisted humor. Examination of conscience; distraction at Mass; meat on Friday. And out there on the Forestville Road . . . He felt himself grin painfully.

"It was after midnight," he said. "Honest, sister. Dewdrop's don't even close up until one o'clock. And I didn't hurt anybody."

"I suppose not yourself," she pointed out curtly. "Oh, no. And I suppose not any family that's waiting and worrying about you—if you have one. Are you a married man, sir?"

"Eight years," he admitted to her. It might help a little. "That's right, sister."

"Children?"

The tone warned him. Eight years? Then a good Catholic family was indicated. He provided one.

"Four of them," he told her. "Two boys and two girls, sister. I feel like a dog."

"I wonder why," she said, after compressing her lips scornfully. "I just wonder, sir. Are any of them old enough to attend here at St. Joseph's?"

But the dark brother proved to be quick enough for her there. She probably knew the name and the family history of every pupil in St. Joseph's. He did not.

"Well, no," he told her. "Not here. I live over to North Falls, sister. That's why I couldn't get home last night. I wanted to see about a job in town, only when I got off the bus yesterday afternoon I met a fellow I knew, and had a couple of beers with him. That's all. That's how it started."

"And I believe," she remarked icily, "we know how it ended, don't we? Just a couple of beers. And wasn't that fine and manly of you? Four small children waiting at home for a bit of food on the table; four innocent little souls entrusted to your care by Almighty God. But what did they matter? Nothing at all, or not to you, sir. A couple of beers! And how long have you been out of work now?"

"Before Christmas," he said. But who was here in the building with her? Why was he wasting time like this? He moved back into the kitchen, where he would have at least a little protection for himself, and again she followed. "I was driving a cab, sister. But they took my license."

"Drinking again?"

He was thinking about the man in the building. He nodded foolishly; and at once, now very knowledgeable and triumphant, she drew herself up against him.

"So," she declared then. "Not only a drunkard; not only a man who broke his pledged word given in front of the church altar. That isn't enough for you. Oh, no. Something else has to be added. You have to prove yourself a cunning and deliberate liar, sir, and by your own admission to me. Not two minutes ago you said that you hadn't had a drop to drink for yourself since last summer. Do you remember that?"

He did. It was exactly what he had said—since last summer. Now even someone like Sister Mary Frances could trip him up. Then what would someone like Frank Rutherfurd do? At that thought, his expression must have become queerly anguished for her, and she was able to catch the anguish, the first honest reaction from him, even if she had no idea of the true reason for it. But it was no wonder that the anguish impressed her. It was genuine enough. They had him, Dillon saw. He was a lost man. It was impossible to stay here any longer; and yet, if he tried to run away through the back door—or, rather, to hobble away—they only had to follow his tracks outside in the fresh snow.

"Oh, you foolish man!" she burst out, again with the hands helplessly fluttering in front of her. "You foolish, foolish . . . You've even hurt yourself. You can't walk right. What in the world do you expect me to do with you?"

But almost at once she must have made up her mind what to do with him. Before he had any chance to stop her, she moved back to the hall door behind them, and called out.

"Oh, John!" she said. "John! Around here, please; to the kitchen. I want you."

John. It was one more time when Dillon found his right hand in his right overcoat pocket; automatic now. John? He backed away from the work table.

"That's all right," he said. "I only twisted my knee a little. Who's John?"

"Oh, yes," Sister Mary Frances said. "Just fine, you are. Stay right where you are, sir. I do believe we have a first-aid kit up in Sister Mary Edward's room."

She vanished, moving away with light daintiness along the school corridor. Dillon made no attempt to stop her. Why bother? It was all useless now. So he remained by the work table, leaning forward against it with his left hand, and watching the door fixedly. Who was John?

He soon learned. When she came back in a minute or so, she had a spryly erect little man with her—long arms, a knobby Irish face, a fold or two of loose skin at the back of his neck, and a red drinker's complexion. As soon as he had marched into the kitchen behind Sister Mary Frances, he winked covertly at Dillon, indicated her back with a forward jab of his right thumb, and by rolling his eyes up piously indicated that there was nothing much to worry about from that quarter. He was even older than Sister Mary Frances. He wore a gray sweater four or five sizes too large for him, and ragged gray pants.

"His left knee," Sister Frances directed. "So get around on the other side of him. Gently now. I want you to help him down to my office."

"Ay-eh," old John said. "Left side. Gentle as a baby, sister. In my time I've helped many a one up the front steps at night. There's a knack, you know. You have to balance them just right."

"I wouldn't doubt it," Sister Mary Frances said. "When they didn't have to help you. Now mind the door, John."

They got him down to the office. It gave him another look out the hall windows, and he could see then that the police cruiser was still over at Dooley's. After they sat him down again, old John helped him roll up his left pants leg. Sister Mary Frances threw both hands in the air.

"Oh, mother of mercy!" she said. "Look at it. Why, it's as big as a grapefruit, John. Here, now. Hand me over the scissors and those two wide rolls of adhesive tape. I'll strap it up as well as I can for him. But I see you're very innocent, the two of you. Total strangers. You don't know each other from Dewdrop's establishment?"

"Ah, how often do I get out now?" old John said. "Past me prime, sister. It's a terrible hard life you lead me."

"Well, of course," Sister Mary Frances said. "Very much abused, aren't you? And don't bother making him any signals behind my back, either. Sister Mary Bernard would know how to handle the both of you and in short order. I'm much too easy. There, sir—" and she finished the strapping. "Try to take a few steps. Is it any better for you?"

It was much better. Now Dillon had a certain support under him, at any rate. He thanked her.

"Oh, yes," Sister Mary Frances said. "Much obliged, aren't you? But now I'm afraid that we have to consider the matter of Mr. Dooley's gas station. You've got to admit the full truth to me. Did you take anything at all over there?"

"Not a thing," he told her; his first honest answer. "I promise you, sister. I never got inside last night."

"Then I suppose we can be thankful for small mercies," she declared sternly. "But don't forget that I'll have to hold myself strictly accountable if you did. Have you your bus ticket back to North Falls?"

He pretended to have it. He glanced down into the pocket of his flannel shirt, and then patted it.

"Right here," he said. "I bought a return, sister."

"Now did you?" she sniffed at him. "Well, mercy me. He bought a return, John. The age of miracles is still with us. All that perfectly good beer money in his pocket, and he bought a return. What time does the bus go out Saturday morning for North Falls?"

"Nine-thirty," old John said. "Just across from the hotel, sister."

"Then I'll take you down there myself when the time comes," she informed Dillon. "And see that you get aboard, too. Don't worry, sir. Did you bother to find out about that job yesterday?"

"I'm coming back," he lied. "The man wasn't there, sister."

"I see." Again the lips were compressed. "You're coming back. But today, of course, you'll have to go home to that poor unfortunate wife of yours with the memory of a grand and glorious night behind you, and the magnificent sum of thirty cents in your pocket. Even John can see how very proud of yourself you are now. Can't you, John?"

"Ah, it's a hard world," old John said, beginning to mop the hall floor with a superbly lackadaisical sweep of the right arm. "If we all had to be proud of ourselves, there'd be no living with some people, sister. Give him a chance."

"Well, I don't know," Sister Mary Frances said, as if coolly deliberating with herself. "I'm just not sure, John. You really think he deserves one?"

"Don't we all?" old John said, again winking at Dillon to indicate that the worst was about over now. "You've driven home the hard lesson to him, sister. You've got the knack somehow. Now maybe it's time for a little Christian compassion."

"The hard lesson," she said, and sighed hopelessly. "Oh, yes. I'm a great one for that, all right. Well . . ."

She took a small steel box out of her drawer, and opened it. Inside Dillon could see a few stamps, a few coins and a few bills. She removed a five.

"But I don't know," she said, as if much uncertain yet. "I just don't know, John. Sister Mary Bernard is going to ask me about this money the first thing when she comes over here today, and what can I tell her? If I thought it would go to those children of his, then perhaps . . . But can I trust him for that, even? He was talkative enough last night, I imagine. He must have put on a regular floor show over at Dewdrop's. But now it's a different story, isn't it? Not a word out of the man; not a straight look, even. What do you think, John?"

"It's all right," Dillon said. "I can manage, sister."

"Well, of course," she said. "Ham and chicken on the table tonight, and broiled steak tomorrow, with thirty whole cents in your pocket. But you'll manage all right. Oh, you foolish, foolish man! Is that all you have to say for yourself? Is that all you're willing to promise me now?"

It appeared so. The foolish man, standing over on the other side of the desk from her, returned her gaze fixedly.

"Then don't promise me," she said, again sighing to herself. "But try to promise your own heart and soul, sir. Make the effort. You're a young man yet, aren't you? Is that so difficult? Now I want no more silly pride out of you. I won't have it, I say. Pick up that money, and try to remember the next time that however often we fall, and we all do, there's a true light for everyone born into this world, sir. Take the money."

"I don't want it," he said. "I don't need it, sister."

"Of course," she replied tartly. "Proud as Lucifer now. Well, it isn't for you, remember, not one penny of it; not a single penny! It's for those children. Now let me see if Chief Rutherfurd has gone yet. Just one moment, sir."

She tip-tapped out into the hall anxiously, both hands held rather high up in front of her, and swaying a little. Old John gave young John a quick nudge in the ribs, pointed down at the five-dollar bill still on the desk and nodded his head vigorously.

"But I do think it's all right," she announced to them. "They seem to be just pulling away over there. Only wait until I make sure that—" A moment or two passed; then she stepped back quickly, and put up a dismayed hand to her lips. "Oh, mother of mercy!" she said. "They are. They're coming in here now. But what do they want? What can I tell them about you? Stay back in that office."

What they wanted, however, was a question only for Sister Mary Frances, not for Dillon. He knew what they wanted. So he could not remain Dillon the thief for her any longer, or Dillon the weakling; he had to be Dillon the murderer again. It had become necessary to announce himself truly.

"Sister," he said. With one hand he took hold of John. With the other, he slipped the service revolver into plain sight for them. "Sister."

"Now please, sir," she whispered back. "Be quiet. I'll have to—"

He moved out into the hall with old John, making very sure that she saw the gun this time; and in doing that, as was instantly understood by each of them, he showed her what at least one man had been able to do with the true light.

"Now you're going to send them away from here," he instructed evenly. "I'm not anywhere around, sister. You never saw me. I mean that. You want anything to happen to John? He's going to stay in your office with me the whole time, and you better remember it. Right here in your office, sister."

Then he could hear Rutherfurd's car coming up the drive. He pulled John in from the hall, shoved him over behind the desk and closed the office door to within two inches. That was at least a small mercy for him. He knew what her expression must be, but it was no longer clearly visible out in the entryway. She had the light behind her, and the sharply pointed shadow of the white coif over her face. Her first movement, after steadying herself against the corridor wall, was to cross herself with her right hand. Her second, once she managed to steady a little, was to come back several steps toward them, or toward John. Because now, Dillon understood, it was only John who mattered to her. There was no one else present in that office any longer for Sister Mary Francis.

"He seems to be very much afraid," she said. "He might do something. So we've got to remember that it's all he can understand, John—to hurt people, and to lie to them. Do whatever he tells you to do. Be very quiet, please. It's all right. I'll send them away for him."

Outside there was the slam of a car door; steps coming up onto the small porch; two voices; the rap of knuckles. But to open the door she had to move out into the entryway, and when she had done that she was all at once beyond Dillon's angle of vision. After that he could only listen to them, but not watch them; her voice, Rutherfurd's voice. Old John, still kneeling behind the desk, blinked up from there in a foolish and bewildered manner.

"You stay down," Dillon whispered. "Do what she told you to do. Keep quiet!"

But what had the other two begun saying to one another? He was unable to hear the words, even by straining desperately, but he could picture a covert gesture from Sister Mary Frances toward the principal's office, and the immediate and understanding nod back that Rutherfurd would return. He had lost control, Dillon realized. Very coolly and cunningly, the dark sister had succeeded in tricking the dark brother. She was not in any personal danger from now on. She could do whatever she wanted to do. Rutherfurd could even have slipped her out at once through the front entry, and yet they still appeared to be talking together. Why? To trick him? Dillon the thief; Dillon the murderer; and now Dillon the fool.

Of course. Obvious. They continued to talk out there, but at the same time they communicated the essential information one to another by sign language. That was the idea. They hoped to keep his attention distracted in this manner while the state trooper got the keys from her, slipped cautiously around to the rear of the building and from that point placed Dillon between two fires. But they could manage it, keeping this conversation going as long as possible, only if he permitted them to; if he was very stupid once more; and if he remained here in the office where Sister Mary Frances had last seen him. Would he remain?

He got old John up from behind the desk. He pushed him on, menacing him in a silent but savage fashion with the service revolver, through the other door in the office, the one that led into the much shorter hall running from front to rear of the building. If he had moved over to the left then, Rutherfurd might have caught a glimpse of him from the vestibule, so he kept right. The broom closet where he had found the mop last night was on the same side of the corridor as the principal's office, just behind it, and he remembered now that the broom closet had only the one door into it, and no windows. Once in there, with buckets and wringers lying about, and two big metal sinks in back, there was scarcely enough room for both of them. He forced John to his knees, so that it would be much easier to handle him, and began to watch the rear end of the hall, and now the extremely dangerous end.

But he now occupied a much better strategic position than in the principal's office. He was completely out of sight from both the front door and the back, or he would be for the first vital second or two, when they finally showed themselves. Rutherfurd, for instance, would have to poke his head around the corridor wall, or out of the office, while the other one would be revealed to Dillon long before Dillon would be revealed to him. There was no way to avoid that. January sun was still streaming in through the rear windows, and also through the glass pane in the back door—the door through which Dillon himself had first peered into the hall last night. It set down, therefore, a warm yellow oblong on the linoleum floor, somewhat lopsided from his position in the broom closet, and yet within sight from there even with Dillon standing a few inches inside, and so fully protected. He would have all the advance warning, then, and all the freedom to act. They would not.

To act in what way, however, and with what purpose in mind? There had been some sort of excuse for what he had done to Frenchy Le Tendre last night, even if no one would believe the excuse. But it was there, Dillon himself knew, and it was true. Yet this time, if he shot down Rutherfurd and the state trooper from deliberate ambush, he would be Dillon the murderer of his own choice. He knew precisely what he was doing now; sufficient reflection, as the catechism handbooks had it, was being vouchsafed to him. Then would he use the gun, if necessary? Was he at last committed to that, even against Frank Rutherfurd?

He put his head against the wall. Now he could no longer hear the two voices out in the front vestibule, and before he could decide about using the gun he heard something else, quite as expected, coming from the other direction—a slow, steadily oncoming crunch of footsteps around the rear of the building. Suppose they forced him to use it? On their own heads, then. He did not want anything like this. But if they . . .

The steps approached closer and closer to the back

door; closer yet. At last, still keeping his head and neck rigid, he slid his eyes around, but it seemed very slowly and effortfully to him, for that cheerful yellow patch of January sunlight out in the hall. It remained blank for a second or two longer; then it did not. He could see the shadow. It was framed for him with the cutout precision of a simulated human target on the police rifle range: a pair of broad shoulders, the pose of a head over them, and even the unmistakable outline of a round cap with the earlaps up, the winter cap of a state trooper. Now?

Certainly the dark brother was all ready for them. John Patrick Dillon, however? He had the revolver pointed straight up along the wall for some reason, and he managed to keep it like that. He waited again. In the meantime he looked down at old John. Old John looked up at him. They were both rigidly motionless. The back door was tried, and tried audibly.

"Oh, Jaysus!" old John whispered to him, peering up fearfully from the store room shadow. "Don't be a damned fool, man. What the hell good is all this, whatever you did? They've got you!"

And they did have him, Dillon realized. Once he showed himself out in the corridor they had him from the back door and from the front door; while on the other hand, if he waited here in the broom closet, they had only to call for two or three more police cars, and a supply of tear gas. He made up his mind then. He gestured with his left hand at John, to remain down and quiet, and faced the corridor. He no longer had the service revolver against the wall, pointed straight up. He was watching the shadow.

But he watched it with an idea that he was no longer in full contact with himself; no body under him, no sensible mind operating. Why should they rush anything, however? All at once the patch of sunlight was again empty, very bright and cheerful in appearance; no shadow any more. And he could hear the footsteps moving away, crunch after crunch, as if they intended to proceed around the other end of the building now, then back to the front steps and Frank Rutherfurd. So he had missed his one chance against them. He had made himself a bigger fool than before. They still had everything in their favor; all the odds. And what did he have? Nothing, no one; only old John.

Old John?

He had almost forgotten about him. He wet his lips quickly; then, with what he felt as another inordinate physical effort, glanced back over his left shoulder.

"Now be God, no!" old John whispered, trying to push himself up hurriedly. "Easy on, can't you? There's no need to lose your head about this. What the hell did I ever do to you that—"

So it was all perfectly understood between them. Old John must have seen the dark brother naked in Dillon at that moment as Dillon himself had begun to feel it naked. She had been given her chance, hadn't she? She heard what he had said to her. Then the moment one of them set foot in this hall. . .

"You turn your head!" he commanded breathlessly. "Do what I tell you to do. Close your eyes, John!"

"And is that how you'd like it?" old John whispered, even fiercer than Dillon now. "You mad dog, you. You filthy, murdering swine! Oh, no! Face to face here. Do your damnedest to me, God blast you—but you're not getting her back here into this building. Go ahead. What are you waiting for?"

John Patrick Dillon did not know; could never have explained to anyone. He waited, however; waited until in the end it was not old John who found it necessary to close his eyes in that broom closet, but young John. But

144

when he opened them, he was quite ready again. There was no choice any longer. He had to end it now, and there was only one way in which it was possible to end it. So he fired his first shot, his second shot and his third shot. Then he walked out into the hall, gun at his side.

But there was only one person to be seen there, Sister Mary Frances. Not so quick and easy, he understood then; not ended for him at all with Rutherfurd and the state trooper blazing away after those three shots the instant he showed himself. One should have been at the back of the hall for him, and one at the front. They were not.

Behind him a wisp of thin, grayish smoke drifted out of the broom closet. He glanced back at it, then at Sister Mary Frances. There was a sudden and almost unbearable physical weakness in him. He pointed the gun for her.

"In there," he announced. "Look for yourself. He's all right. I thought you had them waiting for me, that's all. You think I want to go on like this any more? The hell with it. I've had enough. I only fired those shots to warn them I was coming out. I've had all I can take. What did they tell you about me?"

It was suddenly the most urgent of questions for him. He had to know. But old Sister Mary Frances, very pale now, very quiet, kept her head painfully averted from him. She groped her way down the corridor wall to the broom closet, and said something to old John. He answered her. Then he came out of the closet, and she rested one of her hands on his arm, and began to pat it shakily. When she had done that, she could face Dillon at last, but she was not Sister Mary Frances any more.

"Who you were," she told him. "What you did last night. And then I lied to them—but not for you, sir, and not for myself. All they wanted was to check the doors and the windows in here. Should I thank you for John?"

But it was not enough for Dillon. He had to be told everything that Rutherfurd had mentioned to her; everything she thought now.

"Well, you're going to understand about that," he insisted passionately. "You think I'm no kind of a human being any more? I had my reasons for last night. You look at me!"

Then she did look at him, but in a way that no one ever before in his life had looked at John Patrick Dillon. It was not hatred, which the dark brother would have felt quite ready to return in kind to her. It was not contempt. But it was at once unendurable to Dillon, not to be tolerated.

"So you had your reasons," she said. "Yes. I imagine you did. Very compelling reasons. But without warning; without the chance for an Act of Contrition, even; through a window. May God forgive you for that, if He can. Through a window."

It was a queer thing about the dark brother. When Dillon wanted him, he was nowhere around; when he didn't want him, he was right there. Now it was certainly the dark brother who put his hand on her arm, and once again forced her around to him.

"That's right," he said. "Through a window. But I tell you I had it all planned last night, every bit of the thing. You're going to listen to me, sister. I'm a cop myself. I know how to do these things. So first—"

Useless. Too long; too involved. He was being very stupid again. He gave it up.

"All right," he said. "Maybe I don't care about that, either. Did they drive back into town just now?"

A single nod of the head for him, quiet and composed, with the eyes lowered; no word. He set his teeth.

"Or maybe you think I'm sorry for it," he began jeering at her; the dark brother again. "Well, like hell I am. It's what he deserved."

"Oh, I know that," she said quietly. "You're not sorry. And that's the last horror for you, isn't it? What you can't face. Because if you were sorry . . . But what do you want from me? What are you asking for? Get down on your knees. Pray to God, sir. It's your one hope."

He discovered that he was still holding the service revolver, even though it no longer had any meaning for them. There seemed to be other matters. He put it back into his overcoat pocket.

"This isn't over with," he threatened her. "And you can tell Rutherfurd. Where's the key to this broom closet?"

She wore a wide black belt with a metal ring on it. Now she removed the ring, selected one of the keys and held it out to him, all silently. Old John growled and muttered behind her, glaring at him.

"No, please," she said. "Please, John. We can't reach him now. He won't let us. We can only pray for him. The Jeep key is still in the switch, sir, and Sister Mary Bernard won't be over here from the convent until ten o'clock. You have until then. And now if you won't put your hand on me again, or touch me. Thank you."

She moved back into the broom closet with old John, and Dillon locked the door after them. It was a quarter past nine now, and so he had just forty-five minutes of grace, he understood. How to use them? He hobbled out quickly to the front vestibule. From there he saw deep tire marks in the snow where Rutherfurd had backed the police cruiser around, but the Jeep was still in position. Below him a big yellow truck was barreling along on the state highway for North Falls, and over on the other side of the road Poor Old Charley was pumping gas into a Mustang convertible.

Forty-five minutes. Even from the vestibule he could see that it was a very old Jeep, indeed, and with a manual drive. Then how could he shift properly? It was his left knee that was out of kilter. The Jeep would be quite useless to him. He looked back at the broom closet one last time—a dull, heavy look. Then he dropped the key to it on the linoleum floor, opened the front door to St. Joseph's and walked out.

CHAPTER *7*

He had no positive idea in his head as to any further
action at that moment. He was all done, Dillon felt; no
use any more. But beyond Dooley's he could see the
lake, flat as his palm, white as cake frosting, and a mile
or so toward town, over on the other side, the big green
and white house of Mrs. Roy Vinson, Sr. It again made
him painfully aware that no matter how John Patrick
Dillon felt at this moment Number Two was still waiting for him, and that only the fully completed act could
justify in any way what he had already done to
Frenchy Le Tendre.

He stopped just back of the Jeep, glanced dully again
at each end of the highway before him and lit a cigarette. But now after old John, he was beginning to
understand that he had not pushed his original progres-

sion quite far enough. If it still had to be Number One, and Number Two, then it would have to be Number Three, also—John Patrick Dillon. That was the only answer here. When he had fired those three shots of his in the broom closet, he had wanted and expected Rutherfurd to shoot him down the instant he showed himself in the school hall; but now he saw that he would have to manage that for himself, unfortunately. Surely there could be no problems at all for him if he put down his money now, and made his choice. Number One; Number Two; Number Three. And it would of course be much better for everyone concerned that way. *Finie la guerre,* all right and John Patrick Dillon, too. Now he knew. He would do what Sister Mary Frances had told him to do. He would get down on his knees, and put his own gun in his mouth—but after Number Two. That had to be done first. But in what way?

All of this seemed calm, sensible procedure to him. He reflected a moment, watching Poor Old Charley attend to the Mustang, and then strut back to a small garage in the rear with his usual cockiness. Just me and the cat, Dillon remembered from their conversation yesterday; drop in again, buddy. Well, why not? Another sanctuary was required now. The only possible one was that offered to him by his old friend from Jerome Avenue.

He managed to rouse somewhat. Could he make it over to Dooley's without being seen? He decided he could. There were no immediate neighbors to take note of him. St. Joseph's was the only building on this side of the road. On the other, adjoining the gas station, he saw nothing more than a small gift shop closed for the winter, and a huddle of desolate and deserted wooden cabins; the Idle Hour Motel.

So he watched his chance. As soon as there was no

traffic coming along from either direction, he hopped quickly although clumsily down the hill, remembering to keep in the exact center of the deep ruts, got over to the other side of the state highway with still no cars anywhere, and from there slipped around to the garage that Dooley had just entered. The knee hurt him savagely again after that crazy rush. He had to rest. But he seemed to have made it all right. He heard no sudden commotion out on the road, and heard no blare of a police siren. They were at least two miles from the town proper out here, and when he looked back from the garage the road was still empty.

He entered the garage, as quietly as possible, through a small service door set in the big overhead one. Then he could see Poor Old Charley standing over by a long work bench at the far end of the building, his back turned. He did not hear Dillon come in. He appeared to be checking something, or looking for something, in a big tool box. There were two old cars in the garage, one with the hood gaping, and the other with its back end jacked up. They gave Dillon excellent cover. He was not heard or seen until he was directly behind the other man. Then Charley turned, to squint up into the end of a dirty or clogged fuel pump, saw Dillon, saw his service revolver, and went sick, ugly yellow; so yellow, in the light from the big overhead window, that the freckles stood out against him like black ink spots.

"Now first," Dillon began with him, knowing that he would have to handle this business in quite another way than with Sister Mary Frances; dropping considerably down in class this time, as the tout sheets put it. "First, Charley. Stand right where you are against that work bench, and keep quiet. That's the boy. I only want to talk to you about something. But would you say that I have a hell of a lot to lose now, whatever happens? Take your time, though. I don't want to rush you, Charley. You're getting about three seconds."

One proved altogether sufficient between them. Dooley popped his eyes down at the service revolver, squeezed up as far as possible against the work bench and shook his head violently.

"Then that's fine," Dillon said, still quietly ominous. "Quick thinking, Charley. But there's no reason to get excited about anything. All I want is a little simple information from you. What's going on around town this morning? Has Frank Rutherfurd been out here to talk to you yet?"

It was of course a very old trick with Detective Dillon. Always, when you put the first question or two, you tried to know the correct answers to them; and then, if a lie was attempted by the other party, and at once proven against him, the rest of the interview might be a little more truthful on that side. So this mention of Frank Rutherfurd was the first test between them, and Dooley flunked it.

"You mean here?" he said, putting a weak, anxious grin on his lips, and still watching the service revolver. "Well, no. Of course not. What would he be coming out to talk to me for? I wouldn't give them people the time of day, Johnny, and they know it. Holy Hell! I got nothing against you. I keep my mouth shut about stuff like this. Ask anybody around here. They'll tell you. I'm a right guy."

"That so?" Dillon said. He still felt a bone-dragging physical weariness after old John, but he managed to draw back the service revolver, as if getting ready to slash Dooley across the face with it. "They will, eh? You lying little rat! He was out here with a state trooper not twenty minutes ago, and I saw him. What was he asking you?"

"Asking me?" Dooley squeaked, at once utterly confounded by this direct knowledge against him. "Well, nothing," he babbled. "If I saw you around, Johnny. If I knew— Because of course I had to tell him a little something about how you stopped in here yesterday; about the snow tires. But that's all, honest to God. What would you come after me for? What did I do? I had to tell him. Don't go losing your head, will you?"

"Then don't make me," Dillon warned him. "Just keep it in mind, mister. You tell me the truth now, or I'll show you the kind of guy you are in my book. How about the road over to North Falls? You heard them talking. Have they got it blocked off yet?"

"Well, I don't know," Dooley said, still trying anxiously to placate him. "But maybe they do. What do you think I care about Frenchy Le Tendre, though? Holy God, Johnny! I hated the bastard, and he hated me. He owed me more than two hundred bucks for some work I did on his old Chrysler. I couldn't tell you the last I spoke to the guy, not in months. Listen, will you?"

And last night in the Sachem Room, Dillon remembered, Poor Old Charley had been just as emotional in declaring what friends he and Le Tendre were; how they did everything together. There was never going to be a weaker reed for him to depend on in these circumstances than Poor Old Charley. He gritted his teeth. The knee was still bothering him.

"I'll listen when you say something!" he told Dooley. "What I'm asking you about are the roads. Who's watching them today?"

"You mean to North Falls?" Dooley said. At once his gaze flickered, as if to consider the best answer here for Poor Old Charley; and of course he found it. "Well, I think you'd have a damned good chance to get through," he added then, becoming eagerly persuasive in manner. "Nothing to it, Johnny. I heard them talking about that. Rutherfurd figures you probably headed down for Albany or Utica last night. That's where they're looking."

Which might be true enough, Dillon told himself, if they had not located the police cruiser yet. But at ten o'clock Sister Mary Bernard would arrive at St. Joseph's from the school convent, and then Rutherfurd would know much better, cruiser or no cruiser; still in the neighborhood.

"Then I'll tell you what we're going to do," he announced. "Because that's pretty good news, Charley; I mean how easy it all is. You're going to take me over there in your truck. Then if they're still watching the road, they'll have a pretty good chance to get me, naturally, but I'll have an even better one to get you. So come on. I've wasted enough time. Get your truck started."

It was immediately obvious, however, that the road to North Falls was under the closest possible police surveillance, and that Dooley knew it. He began squeaking again.

"Well, I'd sure like to," he piped shrilly. "But I couldn't. I couldn't, kid. Look at the truck there. I've been working on it all week. We'd only get stuck out on the road somewhere."

"Then get your car," Dillon told him. "No problem, Charley. You've got it sitting right out front, haven't you?"

"What?" Dooley said. And after that there followed a dead pause between them; no other excuse to offer. Dillon grimly permitted it to go on for five or six seconds; then he lifted the service revolver once more, and Poor Old Charley cringed down into the work bench.

"So they're not watching the road," Dillon said. "Okay, Charley. But I'm warning you this time. Pretty easy way to get rid of me, wasn't it?"

"No, no," Dooley protested; the pathetically weak smile again, the anxious and placating head shake. "Why would I do anything like that against you, Johnny? Only . . . only they could be watching it, at that. I don't know. They never said in here."

"Neither will I," Dillon promised him. "Not the third time. Stay right where you are, Charley."

He indicated the spot. Dooley, sweat glistening on the thin, sallow cheeks, eyes fixing hard and bright as a bird's on the service revolver, remained glued to it. Back of them there was a strip of glass set in the big overhead door at eye level, and it permitted Dillon to see that everything looked as quiet and empty as before out on the state road. He came back from the door, sat down on a rickety wooden chair by the work bench and got out his last package of cigarettes. It was empty.

At once Dooley bestirred himself. He appeared to be over his first panic now, and so he got out his own cigarettes with flurried eagerness.

"There," he said. "There you are, kid. Keep them. I got a machine over in the station. Go ahead. Anything else you want me to get, just say it. Anything. Don't think I blame you a damned bit for what you did to that lousy Frenchman, because I don't. You got a lot of people on your side up here, more than you think, Johnny. Yes, sir. They know why you did it now."

And of course they did know, Dillon told himself. Poor Old Charley had called him two or three times by name already; he was fully identified by this time. Which meant, on the face of it, that he could never get as far as five miles from Hazard Lake today in any direction. The cabin over in North Falls was beyond reach. It was Dooley's or nothing for him.

But little by little, he warned himself. The right guy from Jerome Avenue would have to be managed with a very delicate touch, and led on carefully. He must be made to see that with just a little gumption on his part it was not Poor Old Charley at all between them, but Poor Old Johnny. So he took the cigarettes, and lit one.

"Well, thanks," he said. "And all those friends of mine are pretty good news to me, because I could certainly use a couple. You down with them on the list, Charley?"

"You don't even have to ask," Dooley said, managing to sound manfully sympathetic with that statement and yet honestly regretful about it at the same time. "Only wish there was something I could do for you, kid. You're on a hell of a spot, all right."

"I know," Dillon said. "And anybody would be taking a pretty big chance to help me out of it. But I never forget a right guy, Charley, or forgive a wrong one."

"You and me," Dooley agreed with him. "You and me, kid. But I have an idea that you're going to make it out of here all right, Johnny. I've got that feeling, see? You'll think of something."

It might—Dillon was not altogether sure yet—have been an invitation from Poor Old Charley, and of course a very delicate one, too, on his part, to start thinking of something. Had Poor Old Charley seen all that money in his wallet yesterday, when he had paid for the snow tires? He had missed very little else, at any rate. Dillon considered a moment, studying the thin, foxy face, very innocent now, while still holding the service revolver across his knees.

"Sit down," he announced finally. "I don't have anything against you either, Charley. You do all right with this place? How's the gas station business?"

"Oh," Dooley said. He tried to get a little of his old jauntiness back, shrugging his left shoulder so as not to admit anything, and not to deny anything. "A buck here and a buck there," he said. "Nothing to brag about.

You know how it goes, Johnny. Sometimes I'm hopping in and out of the joint all day. Then other times I won't have ten customers until I close up."

"That's the way it goes," Dillon said. It came to him that Poor Old Charley had admired his style yesterday, whatever that was, and so he made an attempt to get it back between them. "You've got to keep your eyes open, Charley. I mean when a good customer comes along, don't miss him. I wouldn't say there's a hell of a lot of them around for you this time of year. But you got a nice little place out here. You ought to be running some kind of sideline."

"I don't know," Dooley said. He shrugged the left shoulder again. "Too far out from town, kid. You mean like selling a little mountain dew under the counter?"

"Or renting a room," Dillon said. His watch showed him that it was twenty minutes of ten; not much time left. "You told me it was only you and the cat, didn't you?"

"Jees, I couldn't," Dooley said. But a wise little grin showed itself, as if he was beginning to enjoy their conversation by this time; his style. "Never even thought of it to tell you the truth, kid. Who'd want to live over a gas station?"

"Well, put an ad in the paper," Dillon said. "See what happens. You might turn out to be a pretty good innkeeper, Charley. You're just the type."

"Always wanted to," Dooley said, beginning to study the tip of his left shoe seriously. "That's a fact, kid. There you hit the nail on the head. It's a pretty small place I got, but I suppose I could put up a real good friend of mine for a couple of days. It would all depend, naturally. I just never thought about it before."

"Of course," Dillon said. "Why should you?" He took the wallet out of his pocket, deliberately riffled through the big wad of bills inside and then tossed a fifty-dollar bill down on the table. Charley's ideal would be a fast man with a buck. "Go on," he said. "Take it, Charley. For the cigarettes, or maybe for the conversation. I'm using up time on you. You know any of the back roads around here?"

"No good," Dooley said, puffing out smoke thoughtfully now, cheeks hollowed. "Of course I do; but so do they, Johnny. I'd sure like to give you a hand if I could. You're my kind of people, see? Not one of these goddam Farmer Johns up here. The trouble is that I can't seem to think of a dam' thing. Or at least—" and he glanced down at the one fifty-dollar bill, as if vaguely and absently, as if he never even considered it lying all alone there on the work bench "—at least not yet, anyway. But I'll keep thinking, kid. You never know, do you?"

"That's it," Dillon said. "Try racking your brains, Charley." He added another fifty. "But I'll tell you what Rutherfurd is going to do," he added. "I'm in the same line myself, remember. If I can keep out of sight up here till Monday or Tuesday, he'll have to give up with the road blocks. He's got to think that I slipped through with the police cruiser last night, because they're not going to find it until next May, the way I see this. Take my word, Charley."

"Wished I could," Dooley said. "Then you'd be just about home, kid. No sweat any more; not for anybody that helped you out, even. But he'll find it, see, no matter what you did with it—and then he'll know. That's the big problem, of course. Because if he couldn't find it, how the hell could he tell where you were? But he'll find it, all right. He got to. He knows this part of the country the way you and me know Fordham Road, Johnny."

"In the auto graveyard?" Dillon said. "Right smack in the middle of two or three hundred old wrecks,

Charley? With the roof emblem gone, with the windshield smashed in, with one of the back doors jimmied off—and with eight or ten inches of snow all over it from front to back this morning? You really think he's going to find it there, Charley?"

"Now I told you before," Dooley said, jumping up out of his chair then, and with a sudden and delighted grin on his face, "and I'll tell you again, kid—I like your style. The goddam auto graveyard! Why, you'll have that farmer running around in circles up here all winter. What gave you the idea, kid? That's something I never would have thought of myself, even."

"Called New York," Dillon said. "But don't tell anybody. It's a secret number we got."

"Then where were you last night?" Dooley whispered. "What did you do? Did anybody see you, Johnny?"

"Not a soul," Dillon lied. "Don't worry about that. You still thinking, Charley?"

He added a third fifty.

"Well, yeah," Dooley said, still grinning. "Thinking like hell, kid. You're going to make it, all right. You know what I figure? You just have to stay put for a couple of days, nice and comfortable. Then you get a friend of yours who drives a truck, maybe, and he just locks you up in the back, and throws an old tarp over your head, and four hours later he could drop you off down in Albany clean as a whistle. You know anybody who drives a truck, kid?"

"Trying to remember," Dillon said, and put down a fourth fifty. "But if I did, Charley, I'd hit him with this much right now, and as much more when he got me down to Albany next week. You ever have to go down there for a load of tires or anything?"

"Oh, now and then," Dooley said, cackling a little, and very gently pulling at his right ear with thumb and forefinger. "Now and then, kid. Only I don't like to, a hell of a lot. All I have to do is to call in, and they deliver the stuff right to my door, see?"

"Of course," Dillon said. "They would, wouldn't they? I forgot that. Well—"

"But I could," Dooley said, now very earnest and helpful in tone, and pulling at the left ear. "It's a funny thing. Sometimes I do, kid."

"No good," Dillon said, counting the fifties. "I'll call New York, Charley. Forget it."

"Okay," Dooley said, watching every flick of the bills covertly. "Whatever you want, of course. Don't think that I'm trying to hold you up, kid. I ain't that kind."

"Oh, I know," Dillon said. "A right guy, Charley. You told me already. Just forget it."

"No, no," Dooley said. "Wait a minute, hah? The only thing is that I'd feel like a skunk taking that money from you. You might need it yourself, kid."

"No, no," Dillon said, right back at him; his turn now. "Never try hustling a hustler, Charley. It's bad business. I thought they learned you that back on Jerome Avenue. You might just wind up getting your brains knocked out."

"Well, Jees," Dooley protested. "Jees, kid. Lemme think, will you?"

"All the time in the world," Dillon said, dropping that admired style of his for the moment, and fixing Dooley with a hard, upward glare. "I'll give you the same three seconds we started out with, Charley. You finished thinking yet?"

"You know something?" Dooley grinned down at him. "Just about, kid; just about. Quite a coincidence, hah? Lemme take a look around the station first, to make sure. Then I'll signal over to you, and leave the back door open. But you'll make it, all right. And I told you I had that feeling, didn't I? Right now you got your name down in the book at Dooley's hotel, kid. You just registered."

So it was at last managed in that way, with barely enough margin, so that it was almost ten o'clock on the nose when Dillon found himself safe and unseen over in Poor Old Charley's upstairs apartment. He was just in time, standing behind one of the living room curtains there, to watch a young, stout nun, very vigorous and determined in stride, get out of a small station wagon before St. Joseph's, take a key out of her skirt pocket and unlock the door for herself.

CHAPTER *8*

Not long afterward, Rutherfurd and the state trooper roared out from town, siren screaming. They also vanished into St. Joseph's for half an hour, and then came out with Sister Mary Frances and old John walking between them. After that Dillon moved over to the living room couch, not waiting or indeed desiring to see anything else, and lay down on it.

He was still there when he heard Rutherfurd's voice under him in the station office. He had his sheepskin coat thrown on a chair, and his service revolver in his pocket. But this time, arms back of his head, eyes closed, a little sweat on his face, he left it there.

In ten minutes or so Rutherfurd went away again, and Poor Old Charley trotted upstairs to make a triumphant factual report.

"But Jees, kid," he began anxiously. "You should have told me you were over in the school last night. That put me on one hell of a spot for a while. I almost dropped my pants when I see them pulling in over here. Why didn't you warn a guy?"

"I figured you'd handle him," Dillon said. "Didn't it go off okay?"

"Well, I think so," Dooley whispered. "All he wanted to know was if I saw anything. Well, sure, I says. I saw a guy getting a lift for himself about a quarter past nine, only I couldn't say whether it was you or not, because he was standing behind the car when I looked out, and I couldn't get too much of a look at him. So where did the car go, he asks me. I think around on Pine Avenue, I tell him. Now they figure you pulled a gun on the driver right away, and that you're making him cut over on one of the back roads to Lake Placid. They got out their maps right away down in the office, and began studying them. But how stupid can you get, kid? The guy believed me."

As the guy, Dillon remembered, had believed in someone named John Patrick Dillon last summer. So Frank Rutherfurd and Sister Mary Frances were on one side of the line now, and what on the other? Dillon and Dooley, the old time vaudeville team. Snappy songs and smart patter; the clown princes of Jerome Avenue. So he had made another choice for himself, and this time an altogether deliberate one. Dillon and Dooley . . .

It was a long morning for him up in the apartment; a very bad morning. He discovered Dooley's hotel, three rooms and bath, to be a dim, filthy horror. Two or three paper bags filled with old garbage sat under the kitchen sink, with a mangy black and white cat sniffing at them, and the one hand towel in the bathroom must have been hanging in there since last summer. Dillon, who

164

had all the fussy personal neatness of a thirty-one-year-old bachelor, took only one look at the bedroom, and closed the door hurriedly. The living room was at least a bit better—sagging upholstered couch, empty beer cans scattered around, overflowing ash trays, and a small television set with a big magnifying lens over the glass. He turned it on softly, only there was no news at eleven o'clock, or at twelve; nothing but one blurry station, and an old cowboy movie.

For reading material there was nothing but a stack of old girlie magazines near the couch, some with specific anatomical drawings penciled in. The bathroom was indescribable. Once at eleven o'clock Dooley came upstairs again, and tried to get a small radio going, but it just sputtered and crackled, no matter how he spun the knobs, and he went down to work on it in the shop out back. Now and again a customer drove in; the service bell rang; and it was possible to hear Dooley chirping away. Apart from that it seemed achingly quiet to Dillon. The cat prowled, mewing plaintively. A cheap kitchen clock ticked. Once, about twenty minutes past eleven, another police cruiser raced by for North Falls.

But at least there was plenty of time to think about Number Two, and to discover that John Patrick Dillon was now more savagely determined than ever in regard to him. Without Number Two, obviously, the whole thing would be quite pointless. It would have to be done. But how to do it? Certain protective measures must have been taken by this time, and Dillon the sharpshooter was going to need exact and detailed information as to what they were. Yet there was no chance that he could learn about them for himself, unfortunately. Through somebody else, then? Through Poor Old Charley?

It appeared to be the only possible solution for him. But he would have to be even more careful this time, he decided. The right guy from Jerome Avenue had already proved that he would be quite willing to smuggle a wanted man out of town, so long as it appeared perfectly safe to him; but he would certainly shy away from taking active part in another deliberate execution. Therefore he would have to be led on carefully—cajoled, flattered, persuaded; and he must never realize where Dillon was leading him. At one o'clock then, when Charley came upstairs for a sandwich and a cup of coffee, it was suggested that he knock around town for a couple of hours that afternoon.

"You might be able to help me a lot," Dillon pointed out. "Just try to pick up anything that you can, Charley. Keep your ears open, and stop in at a couple of the joints around town. What time do you close up here on Saturday?"

"Six o'clock," Dooley said. "Sometimes I get Allie Wilson's kid over here to give me a hand, if I want to do anything. Maybe I could get him after lunch, Johnny. You want me to? I'd keep the apartment door locked, naturally. That part would be okay. I always do. But of course you'd have to be real quiet up here. He might hear you."

"Not a sound," Dillon promised him, getting back to that style of his. "Say hello to one or two of the cops, Charley, and give them the old Jerome Avenue con job. I bet a fellow like you could turn this Jerry Brenner around real quick on Main Street, and he wouldn't even know where he was for five minutes. Right?"

Dooley chuckled.

"You're a great Johnny," he said, "in case I haven't told you before, kid. A great Johnny."

"Well, I think we'd do all right," Dillon encouraged him. "You and me, Charley; the old team. But of course don't push it too much. I don't think you'll have to. Everybody will be talking about it. Just listen. Then stop in at the hotel and see if my car is still out on the parking lot; the black Chevy you put the snow tires on last night. Did Rutherfurd ask you any questions about it?"

"Just a couple," Dooley told him. "Sorry I admitted anything at all, kid. What the hell could I do, though? But I'll give it the old try for you today. If I see any-body watching, I'll just walk right by, of course. Let me call the kid now."

He went downstairs again, remembering to lock the apartment door after himself, and made the arrange-ments. At one-thirty the boy came over, and Dooley drove off for town in his old rattletrap sedan. So it was a long afternoon for Dillon, too. Even now he was not sure that he trusted Poor Old Charley to any extent, but the fact remained that he was stuck with him in these circumstances. And then, he comforted himself, if Dooley entertained any idea of backing out on the arrangement between them, he could have done so when Rutherfurd and the state trooper had been out here. It was probably all right. And it would be a lot better if he could get the Chevy back, with Rutherfurd not thinking yet to check every car on the lot back to an individual guest in the hotel. Then he would have transportation once more.

He managed to doze off for half an hour, woke sud-denly when the service bell jangled downstairs, and after the boy went outside padded over to the window in stocking feet. It seemed to be a legitimate customer, however, and so he took the opportunity to glance one way along the road, then the other. It was still a beau-tifully clear and cold January day, with a delicate blue edge of shadow along the woods, and when he saw the sunlight gleaming on the windows of St. Joseph's oppo-site it made him remember how different it had been over there from Dooley's hotel. Everything clean, quiet, polished; a sense of order, of something dedicated and calmly faithful. Even Dillon the murderer had felt that. Well . . .

He went back to the couch. But did he seriously intend to go on with this thing? What good could it do to anyone, even poor little Chris? Brutal; stupid; useless. Old John had shown him. But to turn away with the thing only half done . . . He put an arm over his eyes, dozed off again after a while and woke up the second time at ten minutes past six.

It was by then full night outside, and Charley Dooley had returned from his reconnaissance tour. There was that whiningly chipper voice downstairs, then the clink and bell of the cash register, and the boy answering him. Later, after locking the outside door after himself, and snapping off the big floodlight over his gas pumps, Dooley came up, looking and acting a lot more jauntily assured than he had a few hours ago; now very much in command of things, it struck Dillon.

"But go ahead," Poor Old Charley began, setting down a couple of paper bags on the table. "Help yourself, kid. Bought a bottle of pretty good Scotch for us. Nothing but the best at Dooley's hotel, hah? Afraid I got bad news about the car, though. They spotted it, all right. Rutherfurd even made me identify the tires for him."

"Okay," Dillon said. The car had never been a very substantial hope; there was still Dooley's sedan downstairs, if he decided to leave here later on. "I thought they would. What did you find out about the road-blocks, though?"

"All around," Dooley said. He lowered a rickety brown shade at the kitchen window, and opened the Scotch. "You'd never get out to the town limits tonight, kid. Stick with me. Right now Jerry Brenner said that they're going through all the summer camps around here. They figure you might be trying to hole up in one of them, maybe. Oh, I got plenty of news, all right. Even saw your girl half an hour ago in the hotel lobby. She was talking to Rutherfurd."

"What girl?" Dillon said. He had just accepted a small drink of the Scotch. Now, unable to follow for the moment, he put it aside slowly. "What are you talking about?"

"But I'm telling you," Dooley said, wiping his hands on a filthy dish towel over the sink. "She flew into Plattsburg this afternoon, and then drove over here in a car she hired. I asked Eddie Allen, the clerk, about her."

Then Dillon also sat down slowly. Rita here? He felt a quick, savagely irritable obscurity of mind at the news. But he did not want her, he told himself. He had enough to do to concentrate on Number Two now, and then on Number Three. That part was difficult enough for him as it was. But with Rita here . . . Dooley was still talking away, however. He must have been much impressed by Rita.

". . . what I'd call a damned good-looking tomato," Dillon heard. "I bet you're doing all right for yourself there, Johnny. Enough for forty men and it's all yours, hah? How is it, kid?"

And he had indeed done all right for himself, Dillon remembered, on that reckoning. He got up. The knee felt a bit better; perhaps his rest this afternoon had helped it. The headache, however, felt a lot worse.

"Charley," he said. He did not want to show the dark brother to Charley; he needed Charley; and yet he could feel the presence gathering. Rita to be discussed in this way? Rita to be smirked about man to man with Poor Old Charley? He had become a member of an old and established firm, all right; Dillon and Dooley. "I only asked you about the roadblocks," he said. "Did you talk to Jerry Brenner about them?"

"Well, pardon me," Dooley said, casually revealing the new order of things between them; Dillon the fugitive here, Dooley the innkeeper. "Pretty goddam touchy all of a sudden, ain't you? Now I don't know that I like that a hell of a lot, Johnny. All I thought was that you'd like to hear about her, so I hung around until she went up in the elevator after talking to the big chief. You could see her in there with her head against the cage, bawling to herself. She had everybody in the whole lobby staring at her. That's why I asked Eddie."

But he had never in his life seen Rita break down like that, it came to Dillon; never. They had quarreled bitterly; they had been altogether finished with one another, time after time; but never a tear. That was something else he had done last night on the Forestville Road; Rita crying. The simple and justified act . . .

"You mean she's at the hotel?" he demanded numbly.

"Jees," Dooley said, pouring out another Scotch for himself. "I told you she went up in the elevator, didn't I? Keep the pace, kid. And they got another friend of yours on the top floor, the one they keep all closed off for the winter. Nobody around but them, see? Eddie Allen told me they're going to have two cops up there in the corner room with him all night. Figure that out. You know who I'm talking about, kid?"

But the statement was an altogether obvious one. The kitchen clock ticking away behind Dillon appeared to slow down noticeably; a lot of odd space in between; and then at last the slow and deliberate tick once more. Was it possible that Number Two had been located for him, and this simply, this easily, this beautifully? He could feel Dooley's foxy little brown eyes watching him for any reaction he might permit. He tried to permit none at all, therefore.

"Well, that's nice," he said. "That seems to be a real brilliant idea, Charley. You certainly made the rounds for yourself. Anything else?"

"One trooper out by the front door," Dooley said, "and a couple more of them out at the old lady's place on Lake Avenue. You'd better stick close to the old innkeeper tonight, kid. How would you have handled the thing?"

"Depends," Dillon said. He wanted to think along one line here, the Number Two line, and to converse quite normally with Poor Old Charley about anything else that came up between them. "I had to spend almost three weeks in a hotel last year with a Grand Jury witness; me and a friend of mine named Eddie McManus. There was nothing to do but play three-handed gin rummy the whole time."

"Now that's the life," Dooley winked. "What a racket! You a gin player, are you? Then let's try a couple of hands after we eat. I just brought home some sliced ham and potato salad; hate to cook, kid. How about a beer with it?"

"Fine with me," Dillon said. But he was still thinking about Number Two, knowing the place of shelter by this time, and the method of protection. What would be the surest method of attack against it? The Hazard House, forty or fifty years old, had an iron fire escape at the rear of the building. He had seen it last night, from the hotel parking lot. What did that promise?

He attempted to decide while they ate the potato salad and the sliced ham, and while they played cards afterward in the living room. And Poor Old Charley turned out to be a very good player, indeed. He had cunning and instinctive card sense, and he won hand after hand. He became cheerful and boisterous, and every few minutes he made another trip to the kitchen. Then Dillon would hear the long glug of whiskey out there, the short spurt of tap water. Finally at eleven o'clock Dillon tried to get the late evening television news on, and Poor Old Charley tried, but there were only flickering horizontal lines behind the magnifier, and no sound.

"Don't get much at night," Dooley admitted. "Not in this part of the country. Once in a while Montreal comes in pretty good, though. Well, I'll go into town tomorrow and pick up the papers for you. But you want to know something?" He hiccuped loudly, giving up with the television. "I got me a kid damned near as old as you are, only I ain't seen him in more than twenty-five years, I guess, or his bitch of a mother. I certainly had a pretty lousy life for myself, Johnny. What the hell do you suppose it's all about, anyway?"

Getting philosophical now, Dillon told himself, and soon sleepy; but Poor Old Charley as husband and father was an unexpected angle for him. He tried to pretend interest in it.

"I've tried to figure that out myself," he said. "It's a pretty big question, though. What happened, Charley? The wife leave you?"

"Twenty-five years ago," Dooley said, giving him a solemn nod over the card table. "I got the old con back in '38, kid, and they sent me to a state sanitarium up here, and I spent two years flat on my back. They had to collapse one of my lungs, see? Then finally they let me go down to New York on a visit, when I begin to pull around a little, and when I get down there Dolly makes me sit way over on the other side of the room from her. Afraid of the old T.B., of course. That was it. They were all ignorant people.

"Well—" He made a gesture with his cigarette, trying for the old Dooley cockiness, but not finding it. "She has her old lady there, and her old man, and her two brothers, the whole goddam family, and they all begin saying that they never had anything like that on their side, and that I certainly got a lot of nerve bothering people in my condition. I'm still lousy with it; I'll never be able to make a decent living for Dolly and the kid again; so what the hell good am I?

"So I begin to cry, Johnny. Imagine that, hah? Poor Old Charley. I get all excited. They won't let me see the kid, even. They say he's out somewhere. Then I have to sit up all night in Grand Central Station, no place to go, and when I get back up here I'm spitting up blood again, and I get another two years of it. But that's the last I ever seen or heard of her and the kid, Johnny. Story of my life, hah? I sure picked the right name for this dump, didn't I?"

And this was a second new aspect of Poor Old Charley; no more jaunty defenses up. Funny thing, Dillon found himself thinking. He had always felt himself scornfully justified in despising people like Poor Old Charley—mean, envious, cowardly, hating, the lowest of the low, in fact; and yet it must have been even more necessary for them than for other people to put up some kind of front against life. The front, most of the time, was a very poor one; but what other was available? There was even a front needed now for John Patrick Dillon; a claim of integrity. He had already decided that to go on against Number Two was brutal and quite useless; and yet he was forcing himself to go on, wasn't he?

"Ah, what the hell," Poor Old Charley said, again blinking owlishly. "I guess it's the booze, kid. But you know it's kind of nice having someone to talk to like

173

this. You got a knack, Johnny. You make a guy feel that if he ain't a hell of a lot, maybe, then who is? You make a couple of jokes with him. You're all right."

Yes, Dillon remembered, his style; but he was not very proud of it at the moment. He had made a couple of jokes. He had needed Charley, just the way he had needed Sister Mary Frances this morning. And what had she said when she found out? That all he knew was how to hurt people, and how to lie to them. Any argument there?

"Maybe I'm beginning to realize that I'm not a hell of a lot myself," he admitted finally. "That's it, Charley. Not after last night."

"No, no," Dooley said, very earnest. "I got a lot of respect for you, kid. I mean that. You stood up for yourself. Bang, and right smack through the head. It bother you any?"

"I don't know," Dillon said. They had reached a moment of truth now. He had to grin painfully. A big man in Poor Old Charley's book; but in his own, and in Rita's? "Only I wouldn't say that I'm exactly proud of myself. It wasn't the right way, Charley."

"Of course," Dooley said. "You missed out with the other bastard, and he caused the whole thing. Oh, it's a sad world, kid; sadder than you think. The bottle's empty. Well, that's one quart we knocked off in a hell of a hurry. We do all right together, don't we? You and me, Johnny. You and me."

"Oh, boy," Dillon said. But he had used the reverse of Dooley's method; a lot of tap water, a minimum of whiskey. "We sure did."

"Not even another drop," Dooley hiccupped. "Time to knock it off, maybe. You had a pretty tough day. But come on, kid. I'll share the bed with you. Plenty of room."

"Thanks," Dillon said. He could remember the bed

from the afternoon. "I'll stay here on the couch, Charley. But have a nightcap, if you want. I've got a little French brandy in my overcoat pocket. Try it."

"So what?" Dooley said, testily argumentative all of a sudden. "Big deal, hah? French brandy! Well, I drunk that before. I drunk any goddam thing you can think of. You making a crack or something?"

"No crack," Dillon said. It was only twenty minutes of twelve, he saw, and so there was still plenty of time for that unfinished business of his over at the Hazard House; the later the better, it might be, when Dooley was sound asleep. He tossed the brandy over, and used Johnny Dillon's style again. "You gargle out the front window every morning with that stuff," he said, "and you'll never get another cold as long as you live, Charley. Polishes the tonsils."

Poor Old Charley appeared to think that remark enormously funny. He began to laugh, and laughed until the tears came.

"You know I certainly like your style," he insisted, when he had at last recovered himself. "Gargle it out the front window! Why don't you head for Florida, kid? Maybe I could meet you down there. I mean sell this joint, see. What the hell, I still got a lot of the old viggerish left. You think you're pretty cute, Johnny, but I'm a hell of a lot cuter. We'd do all right down there with your looks and my brains. I tell you now. The first thing is, we'd try to get hold of some old bitch loaded with jack. And then . . ."

He rambled on drunkenly, in a Poor Old Charley daydream, his eyes getting heavier and more glassy at every word that came out of him. Soon the brandy bottle slipped from his hand. He groped for it over the arm of his chair, and then appeared to forget what he was groping for. He yawned; yawned again. At last he put his arms on the table, and his head on them. Dillon smoked quietly, laying out a hand of solitaire opposite. Perhaps twenty minutes went by. At the end of that time, when he risked a first cautious movement out of the other chair, Poor Old Charley was puffing away in slow, rhythmical fashion.

He continued like that while Dillon washed and shaved in the bathroom, afterward checking out the one clothes closet. But there was too great a difference in size between them. Nothing fitted him. Not the Mackinaw, not an old leather windbreaker, and not an old-fashioned, double-breasted dress overcoat that looked as if it must have come from the classiest Bon Ton on Jerome Avenue. And yet Dillon understood that it would be better to find a change of clothes for himself; everybody in town would know about the cap and the sheepskin coat by this time. But of course there was the limp, too, and Rutherfurd would have heard all about that now through Sister Mary Frances. It was useless, then. It could never be done to Number Two. But Number Three, on the other hand, would be quite simple. He had only to walk out into the woods behind Dooley's, kneel down, as Sister Mary Frances had told him to do, and take out the service revolver.

He considered the action very seriously for a time. He sat down out in the kitchen, in the dark there, and thought of a headquarters sergeant who had done it like that over in Central Park. Why involve anybody else in this business? He had involved enough by this time, and certainly he had found out that he could never isolate an act, and keep it isolated, even a simple and justified act. One decision led to another; bad to worse, as Sister Mary Frances would probably have it, and good to better. Why should Rita be tortured any more? Better the clean, final break. Why should Poor Old Charley be put on a hell of a spot for telling him about the Hazard House? And yet—the one person who had started this whole thing was the one person still entirely unaffected by it. Was it even thinkable, then, to let him get off now? Johnny, Johnny . . . Those were the last two words that a sixteen-year-old kid had ever uttered in life. And would Johnny forget them?

So he had come around full circle, Dillon realized; back again to the original starting point. It might be that he did not want to go on with Number Two at all, if he could admit the truth to himself; it might be that he was beginning to understand at last, with poor little Chris dead and buried for six months, how fruitless and insane this all was. But he could not permit any of that to matter to him. The thing had to be done. Only the completed act could represent an undeniable if brutal integrity on his part—the thing begun, and the thing finished. And certainly, if he turned off now, he could never be sure of his own reasons for turning off. Perhaps he was getting a little afraid here, and afraid for himself, with at least three of Rutherfurd's men watching and waiting for him at the Hazard House. That could be it. Was it?

Whether or no, it made up his mind for Dillon. Once again he was able to pump up that sense of deadly purpose and dedication in himself, and welcome it. He got up, waited a moment to hear Dooley still puffing away in the living room and opened the hall door. Then he could see a dim night light on down in the office. He put his own cap on, and threw his own sheepskin coat over his arm. So be it, then. What would happen would happen. He had got as far as the third step down, trying to favor his bad leg carefully, when the bell rang.

CHAPTER 9

There must have been a night buzzer outside. It sent a shrill, jangling peal up through the apartment kitchen behind Dillon, and he crouched down frantically, try-ing to see who it was between the railing slats. But the living room wall came down on that side. He had to hobble down two more steps, and then crouch a second time. There was no car out at the pumps, because he had heard no car. It was not an immediate neighbor, either, because there was none at all here around Dooley's. Then who?

It was a woman, a single woman. He could see that. He could also see a Persian lamb coat that seemed familiar to him, and a gray hat with a perky little red arrow in it. But for a moment he refused to believe what he saw, still crouching helplessly down on the bad knee. He decided to remain where he was first, and not answer her. But then, if he did that, he understood that she would ring the bell again, and perhaps wake Dooley this second time. Already she had stepped back to look up again at the living room lamp, which was still on behind drawn shades, and now she came back to the door again, and rapped sharply, at the same time trying to peer ahead into Dooley's office. So she would ring again, Dillon knew, with the light on up there, and keep ringing. Nothing else for it. He hobbled down the rest of the stairs, gestured over at her to keep quiet and unlocked the door.

He had a glimpse of the state road in front of Dooley's, rutted here and there by glare ice under bitter January starlight, and with the dark shadow of St. Joseph's slanting down across it. But he could see no car, no headlights in either direction and no watchers. Then he locked the door after Rita, hobbled back to the stairs and heard no movement from Dooley up in the apartment. After that there was nothing at all left to do but turn around to her.

And of course she knew everything now. Rutherfurd must have told her. So when she made a movement toward him, Dillon backed off hurriedly, not wanting even the least physical contact between them. He remembered how difficult it had been to announce himself to Sister Mary Frances this morning. He understood at once how much more difficult it would be with Rita now.

"There's someone up in the apartment," he whispered, indicating the open stairway to her. "Keep your voice down. But how did you know where I was, Rita? Who told you?"

It must have been very difficult for Rita, also. When she saw him move away from her she stopped over by the cigarette machine, to one side of the pay phone from which he had called her yesterday afternoon. There, even with the one night light not showing too much, she looked pale, tired and miserably anxious to Dillon.

"When I talked to you yesterday afternoon," she whispered, also glancing over at the apartment stairway. "They had to call you back, Johnny. Don't you remember? Then I heard somebody say to the operator that it was Charley Dooley's place, but I only thought of that when I was trying to get to sleep a few minutes ago. I got his address out of the phone book, and I remembered that the North Falls Road was the way I came in this afternoon. I didn't have to ask anybody. It's all right, Johnny."

Yes, he told himself; fine. But all this was the very simple part of the business for them, about Rita; it was not what really mattered in any way. So he moved back to the front window again, pretending to watch the road anxiously.

"Then where's your car?" he asked her. "Did you drive out here, Rita?"

"Behind the gift shop," she told him. "Just next door, Johnny. And nobody followed me, either. I made sure."

He tried to think of another question for her; anything at all.

"Then get over there," he directed. "Against the radiator. What are you shivering for? Are you cold?"

"Does that matter?" she said. She laid her pocketbook on the radiator with a suddenly distracted gesture, still watching him. "Can't you tell me?" she whispered. "My God, Johnny! What happened up here last night? What did you do?"

He made a slight motion of the head, but without facing her. There were black shadows under the trees, and a faint, cold glitter of winter starlight over on the school windows. Dooley's sign swung in the wind with sudden, scraping raucousness. And now it had to come out, Dillon understood—what he had done. It could no longer be avoided by him.

"But I thought Rutherfurd told you," he began effortfully. "I heard you were talking to him this afternoon. I just couldn't take it any more after he called me Thursday night, Rita. I was the one that let Chris come up here in the first place, and then I just sat around down in New York month after month, not doing a damned thing about what happened to her. Even Loretta told me. So all right, I decided. They weren't going to get away with the thing, either of them. I'd take care of it myself, since nobody else was.

"I admit that. I intended to pay them out, Rita. But I knew how I'd spoil everything for you and me, if I took it into my own hands that way, and so I sat up until three or four in the morning thinking about us. Of course I could come up here and shoot the two of them down in cold blood, if I was that kind of a man. But was I? All of a sudden I understood what I could do and what I couldn't do, even for Chrissy. I wasn't a mad dog, after all. I just couldn't do it that way. Now you won't believe this, I guess, after how it finally worked out for me. But all I intended to do when I came up here, Rita—"

"Tell me," she said quietly, but perhaps not too evenly. "I'd believe you whatever it is. Tell me, Johnny."

He heard her moving over behind him, made a slight gesture to keep her away from Dillon the murderer and caught a reflection of his face in the front window. It looked haggardly shadowed and anxious to him, a true ghost face, with the snow glittering behind it, and a few icy stars that were caught up in the tree branches around St. Joseph's.

"Well, finally I did figure it out," he whispered back.

"Or I thought I did. Maybe I could do it the right way, I told myself, if I could think of how to scare hell out of this Frenchy Le Tendre. Rutherfurd had given me a certain idea about him. So the first thing I did was to hire a cabin over in North Falls, a double cabin, and to tell the clerk that I was registering for a party of four people. After that I came over here and sized everything up, and made what you could call a direct threat against Le Tendre. I had to. That was the whole idea, actually. I had to bluff him into confessing what he'd done, Rita."

Now she was only on the other side of a battered old desk from him.

"But bluff him about what?" she demanded anxiously. "Then you never intended to—to kill him, Johnny? You never had that thought in your head?"

But at the moment that was much too straight a question for him. He knew that he could not answer it either one way or the other for Rita, not in all honesty, and therefore he avoided an answer.

"Well, I brought the rifle with me," he said. "I found out where they were last night, both of them, and what they were doing, and then I drove out to Frenchy's house, and got up close enough in the woods so that I could see him in the living room, and talking to someone. What I figured was that I couldn't miss anything I aimed for, not at that distance, and I could see a bottle of whiskey on the table. Well, I'd hit that, I thought, just close enough to make Frenchy believe I was out gunning for him, after the threat I'd made, and then I'd go back to the hotel and force Vinson to come back with me to North Falls, where I had that double cabin all ready for us.

"That part would have been easy enough. It was a pretty big motel, with a lot of skiing guests for the weekend, and I was going to slip the maid a ten-dollar bill, and ask her not to bother us until Monday. I'd tell her one of the girls was sick. What would she care about cleaning up the cabin then, if we didn't? But it would give me a nice, quiet place to keep Vinson then, and I even bought a lot of canned goods we could eat. I tell you I had it all worked out, Rita. Le Tendre would have to believe that I'd only missed him by an eyelash, but got the other fellow. Where was he, otherwise? What had happened to him? It was bound to be all over town the next morning, I mean the way Vinson dropped out of sight like that. But at the same time it seemed a pretty good chance to me that Frenchy would back off at least a couple of days from telling Rutherfurd about the threat I'd made against him, and the shot I'd fired. He couldn't be positive about who'd done that, because there was another fellow up here who hated him, but I figured he'd sure as hell begin to sweat blood, Rita. He knew what he'd done, and he had a bad conscience. I was depending on that.

"So Sunday night I was going to bring Vinson back here in the car with me, handcuff him out in the woods for a while and then slip into Frenchy's house. I knew he lived all alone, and I knew I could get in easy through one of his cellar windows, so I figured I could be right in his bedroom, and have the service revolver stuck between his eyes, before he had any idea what was happening.

"All right, I'd tell him. Now it was his turn. He was coming out to Mountainview Park with me, just the way I'd made Vinson do Friday night, and then he was going to kneel down in the snow there beside Vinson's body, and I was going to shoot him through the back of the head. He was getting the same dose.

"And I knew it was going to work out for me, if I could do it that way. What do you hear these days but police brutality, Rita? Well, I intended to give him a sample of police brutality, all right, and a lot more than he was going to be able to handle. In about two seconds I knew I'd have had him crying and blubbering for some kind of chance from me. Then I was going to begin cursing and raving like a lunatic, and tell him that Vinson had admitted the whole thing before I shot him, and that he better admit it, too. Where was the money Vinson gave him?

"You see the idea? I knew they'd cooked it up between them; so did Rutherfurd; but we couldn't prove it. And of course it would have been cash business; no checks floating around, or else Rutherfurd would have begun asking questions. So it seemed to me that if Vinson had to pay off in cash, then Le Tendre would have to keep the cash somewhere around the house, instead of putting it in a bank; same reason. Now that was my whole idea, Rita. As soon as I'd scared the true story out of Frenchy, and had the cash money to prove it with, I was going to call Rutherfurd in. I couldn't at first, naturally, because in his position he could never go along with that shot through the window angle, or with kidnaping Vinson. And in the end I knew I'd be in a lot of trouble myself about that part, over the line; but I didn't care any more. I owed something to Chris, didn't I? So that's it. I intended to hand the whole case over to Rutherfurd then, sealed and delivered. Only what happened, actually . . ."

His voice caught, and he turned blindly back to the front window. There was a brief pause.

"I know," Rita whispered then, managing to get hold of his hand shakily. "I know, Johnny. You could never have meant . . . Oh, thank God! It was exactly what you intended. But why didn't you do it in that way?"

He gave her a numb, oddly fixed stare from the eye corners. Dillon the murderer . . . Why, indeed?

"Wanted to," he croaked back. "Started to, Rita. But

remember what you told me once about that dark brother I had? He's around, all right. I found out. It wasn't enough, the way he saw it. They'd only get a couple of years apiece, maybe, and there was poor little Chris still rotting away in Gate of Heaven. They could get Le Tendre for perjury. They could nail the other fellow for suborning a witness, in addition to the other charges against him, but that was it. And suppose because of the way I was doing the things, which was the only way I could think of to do it, I wouldn't be allowed to present the evidence in court, even?

"That only struck me when I was creeping up through the woods last night. I don't know whether you know it or not, Rita, but we have to be pretty careful these days about the way we get evidence. I'd have to come into court with clean hands, I remembered, if I wanted the evidence to hold up; so maybe, even with all the proof against them, they could still twist out of the thing. And that upset me a little. The first thing I knew I wasn't even aiming for the whiskey bottle, but for Le Tendre. Well, the hell with it, I thought. Why not finish the job myself on the two of them, and make sure? What else did they deserve? But I managed to calm down after that, or thought I did. The second time, as soon as Frenchy got out of the way, I aimed for the whiskey bottle. Then I fired.

"I don't know what happened then. Maybe he moved, or maybe I went ahead and did the thing the way I'd been planning to do it the whole time. I couldn't say. But then I thought no, I hit the bottle, all right, only a bit of glass flew up and cut him on the temple. That's why he was bleeding. So I still thought it was okay for me, until I drove back to the hotel and couldn't find Vinson around. Then I didn't know what to do, and I was still waiting when the news came in about Frenchy getting the top of his head blown off. As soon as I heard that, I knew who did it. I did it. I killed him, Rita."

"No," she whispered back fiercely at him. "No, Johnny. How could you, without meaning to? Look at all the medals you've won. It isn't possible, that's all. You just told me yourself. You couldn't do anything like that. You're not the kind."

Perhaps not, Dillon thought. The dark brother, however? Which of them had fired that one shot last night? It was the question he had asked himself over and over afterward in St. Joseph's. There was still no clear answer to be found.

"But that's it," he agreed painfully. "Don't you see? Now I can never claim that it was an accident, Rita. I'm one of the best shots in the department back home. I should have been able to hit a dime at that range. Who'd believe me?"

"Then find out what you did hit," she urged him. "If you're not sure. I'll drive you out to that house, Johnny. Then tell Rutherfurd exactly what you told me. He'll help you to prove what happened. I'll help you. But you didn't do anything to Roy Vinson, did you? They can't find him anywhere. Rutherfurd said they've been looking for him all day."

"He's at the hotel," he explained to her. "Under guard. Rutherfurd isn't blatting it around, that's all; not until he has me located. You can't blame him. But if I could only remember what I hit, Rita! That's what scares me so much. The whole room went pitch black; then I ran. All I know is that there was somebody else in there, and that Frenchy was talking to him. A big fellow, too; big as Vinson. I saw his shadow."

"Then maybe that's who it was," she whispered. "They might have have had plenty to talk over, Johnny

—with you in town. Maybe you did scare this Le Tendre. Maybe you scared him so much that he wanted to back out on the whole thing. How do you know?"

At first it was just Rita trying to hearten and encourage him with nothing more than a forlorn hope, an altogether absurd hope. But then it wasn't. Number One and Number Two might indeed have set up a nice, quiet little meeting last night, with Chris Dillon's brother in town, and openly announcing himself. They would certainly have had plenty to talk about. And then what? Then Dillon the sharpshooter might have fired as accurate a shot through that window as he had ever fired on a police rifle range, and permitted the other man in that room to finish the job on Frenchy, the real job!

"God Almighty!" he got out, in a slow, dazed manner. "Wait a minute, Rita. I think you've got something. You know what I did last night, if I hit that whiskey bottle the way I wanted to, and not Le Tendre? I gave somebody else a chance at a free killing. Just look at the thing. The both of them must have thought I was trying to kill Frenchy, only with the lamp being knocked over I couldn't tell whether I did it or not. But I was sure going to believe that I had, if he was killed. Let me think a minute. Vinson was looking at his watch in the hotel taproom. I saw him. Suppose he had an appointment with Frenchy?"

And quite suddenly he was Detective Dillon again; no more dark brother. The black pall lifted. Detail after detail begin to fit into clear focus for him. A free killing, indeed—and everything solved with just a little quickness and determination on Number Two's part. What looked like a legitimate attempt had just been made on Frenchy Le Tendre's life; so why wouldn't Number Two have gone ahead and finished the thing? No worry about Frenchy backing out then at the last moment; no worry about paying out more hush money year after year with the kind of hold that Le Tendre would have against him. And more than that, even—no further concern on Number Two's part about a private vengeance being taken by Chris Dillon's brother, as a private vengeance had just been apparently attempted against Frenchy Le Tendre. He could do the thing neatly and safely, and who would be blamed for it? Who, for that matter, was going to believe that he himself had actually done the thing?

There was only one answer to those questions—John Patrick Dillon. At one stroke, Number Two could make himself free and clear for the rest of his days— Frenchy's story on record, Frenchy's mouth closed once and for all, and Chris Dillon's brother crazily on the run. Not Dillon the murderer at all, then; but Dillon the fool, rather. Who had been the other man in that room?

He managed to rouse himself.

"I'm going out to the Forestville Road," he told Rita. "I want to take a look at that room out there. If I hit that whiskey bottle, then I didn't hit Frenchy. You stay here and wait for me. It's all right. Dooley's sound asleep up in the apartment. I won't be ten minutes, Rita. I've got to know about this!"

"You're not going without me," she said. "Not without me, Johnny. I'll drive you."

"But you've done enough," he whispered. "Good God, Rita, you're going to be in all kinds of trouble if Rutherfurd finds out that you were even talking to me. Let me drop you off near the hotel, anyway."

"I'll always be where you are," she said. "Always, Johnny. Now come on."

She gave him no choice. The next moment she was outside the door, and when Dillon followed her she put her arms around him, and kissed him. They clung together, two shadows in the open area around Dooley's gas pumps. It was another great help for Detective Dillon. A minute later they were in her car, the two of them. The upstairs light was still on in Dooley's apartment when they drove by, and the shades down. St. Joseph's, dark and quiet up on the hill, had just the tip end of a new moon showing behind it.

CHAPTER *10*

It had been numbingly cold during the snowstorm last night. Now it seemed to Dillon that there was only a difference of kind out in the open, but not of degree; what he felt even in the car was a thin, penetrating cold, quiet as stone, hard as crystal. Over the lake a glittering array of remote heavenly constellations could be seen, crust beyond crust. They blazed down silently on the car, giving the air an effect of transparent blackness; on the dark, frozen woods, on the glitter of fresh snow, and beyond the woods on an undulating dim line, ghost quiet, of slopes and ridges. Once they were past Dooley's he could see the illuminated clock on the Town Hall, and on higher ground to the left a few scattered small lights up on Franklin Avenue. The time was twenty-five minutes of two Sunday morning.

But that whiskey bottle, he was asking himself; smashed or not smashed? He felt that he was still very badly uncertain about it. First he would be convinced that the whiskey bottle had disintegrated faster than thought at his one shot, and then that it had remained in place on the end table, erect and unmarked, when Frenchy had knocked the lamp over. So in one case he would be Dillon the murderer even yet; but in the other, and beyond question this time, Dillon the fool. Which?

Yet there had been no time at all to think it out for himself last night in the Sachem Room, after the news came; time to run, only. A single rifle bullet had been fired by him through that window, and Frenchy Le Tendre had been shot dead; but only now was he beginning to realize that those actions might not have been two equal parts of the same deadly result. At least forty-five minutes had elapsed after he had got back to the hotel from the Forestville Road before that town cop had appeared looking for Frank Rutherfurd, and a good many things might have been arranged by Number Two during that period. He might have left the Sachem Room immediately after Dillon had left it, and driven out to the Forestville Road while Dillon was still waiting over in that other tavern for Frenchy to get well settled; and so have been in the Le Tendre living room, with the shade carefully pulled down to conceal his presence, by the time Dillon arrived.

So that fitted—the time element. And what had the bartender at the hotel said, when Dillon had asked him about Number Two? That he had left only a little while ago. But how long was a little while? The term was altogether indefinite. It might have been twenty minutes, or forty minutes. Who could say? Number Two still appeared to be leading that charmed life of his. If Detective Dillon had only been alert and suspicious

192

enough last night to keep pushing the bartender, a definite time might have been set. Now it was too late for that, probably. The bartender would not be positive at all. Too much had happened immediately afterward when Dillon the murderer, or else Dillon the fool, had found himself racing out of the Sachem Room in blind, stupid panic.

But all that could be decided later. Just now it was necessary to establish, one way or another, if Detective Dillon had hit that whiskey bottle, and if a personal meeting had indeed taken place between Number One and Number Two. But if one had, what better spot could have been found for it than the Le Tendre house? Only Frenchy there; no close neighbors; everything quiet and private between them.

And there might have been extremely important business on the agenda. Perhaps Le Tendre had wanted to back out on the whole arrangement then, with Chris Dillon's brother threatening him, or perhaps he had tried to hold up Roy Vinson for a little more money. But certainly, if any serious differences had come up, then the shot through the window had presented Number Two with a golden opportunity to rid himself once and for all of Number One. He had always been the risky link in the chain, as Detective Dillon had understood almost at once. Then why wouldn't those cool, shrewd and watchfully aloof gray eyes of Number Two have understood it a lot better, and a lot quicker?

So presume that they had met last night to discuss something or other, whatever it was. Then a shot, apparently fired with the most deadly intent, had just missed Le Tendre, as it was meant to miss him; but Number Two could never have suspected that part. From his viewpoint, it must have appeared to be a perfectly bona fide attempt against Frenchy's life, and he might have proved quick enough to take instant advan-

tage of it. Who had threatened Le Tendre earlier in the evening? Chris Dillon's brother. And who had fired that shot through the window at him? Obviously the same man. He was a man, therefore, who could be led to believe that he had succeeded in his attempt; a man who would never think of accusing anyone else; and most important of all a man who might be shot down in a few hours by Rutherfurd's people as an armed, desperate fugitive. And then who was going to quibble about a rifle bullet being found in Frenchy Le Tendre's living room wall, and another bullet, from a different gun, in Frenchy himself? It would be assumed that he had used two weapons, and at once discarded the fatal one. He was a police officer himself, after all. He knew the angles, and had come well prepared.

But now the first village light had appeared for them over the Bridge Street intersection. On their right, two blocks ahead, was the Hazard House, and on their left, curving around the lake, River Street led directly past the Town Hall to Franklin Avenue. They kept left, heading for the blinker light at the next crossing.

"When you talked to Rutherfurd," he asked Rita hurriedly, "did he say who called in from Le Tendre's last night? Somebody must have. It wasn't Vinson, was it?"

"I couldn't say," Rita admitted. "He didn't tell me. But maybe it was, Johnny."

And maybe it wasn't. No. Number Two would never be that much of a fool. He would know much better than to voluntarily place himself anywhere near the Forestville Road last night. Then who had called the Hazard Lake Police Department? He would have to find out about that, too. Detective Dillon was starting behind scratch on this thing.

And now they had reached the blinker light on Main Street, with Rita slowing up carefully and properly for it. She stopped briefly, too, and when she did they

could both look over at the Town Hall, and see the three men who were getting into a police cruiser there, and in pretty much of a hurry. The three men, Dillon could see now, were a town cop, a state trooper and Frank Rutherfurd.

"Let them get past," he whispered, at once crouching himself down in back of the dashboard. "Did they see you? Did they recognize the car, Rita?"

But then he remembered that it was a hired car, and that Rutherfurd had never seen it before. He did not appear to recognize Rita, either. So the police cruiser whipped by them in one direction for the Hazard House, and after it had gone past Rita turned off in the other direction for Franklin Avenue.

"It's all right," she whispered shakily. "They never paid any attention to me, Johnny. I think they're going down to the hotel."

They were, and very fast, but without the siren. Dillon watched them through the back window, He saw them pull up in front of the hotel, and jump out again, all three; then Rita made the turn onto Franklin Avenue. He could see nothing else after that.

"It's that skunk Dooley," he explained breathlessly to her, more and more Detective Dillon now. "He must have heard us leave back there, Rita, and figured you were taking me to the hotel. He's the one told me about Roy Vinson, and he's scared stiff about what he thinks I'm going to do to him now; so he called in. He's the only one that could have called in. Oh, he's a right guy, all right. The dirty little . . ."

But that seemed to be the dark brother again, and he got it under control quickly. The Franklin Avenue hill dropped back. Ahead of them now he could see a few lonely street lights, and behind them that big illuminated clock over the Town Hall. An irregular long row of icicles hung over the roof gutters, like the jocose up-and-down grin on a Halloween pumpkin, and here and there powdery white drifts of snow had tumbled out into the road, where a driveway exit had been cleared off, or a car had struggled to get away from the curb, leaving behind a welter of deep, frozen ruts. But at two o'clock Sunday morning they saw no traffic, no people and no house lights along Franklin Avenue, and in another minute or so they had reached the Forestville Road turnoff.

"Now I want you to wait for me in the car," he insisted to Rita. "All I have to see is whether I hit that whiskey bottle or not. It won't take me five minutes."

"If you'll be careful," she said, still a bit shaky. "Promise me, Johnny. Just look in through the window. But you don't have to prove anything to me, remember. I know what happened."

Maybe she did, being Rita; but it would certainly be required, Dillon understood, to prove point after point about this to Frank Rutherfurd. But grant that he had hit the whiskey bottle last night, and not Le Tendre. Then what had happened? His bullet must have smashed straight on into the living room wall, which meant that as soon as the lab reports came back Rutherfurd would find out that he had two different bullets to puzzle over, fired from two different guns. One of them had killed Frenchy, if Detective Dillon was right. The other, the one from his rifle, had not.

Then why had two guns been fired? Surely Rutherfurd could be made to understand that no one would have remained sitting in that window after a first bullet had just missed him. Even a complete idiot would have known what to do in a situation of that nature—duck down. The reaction would be immediate and instinctive. Then how could Dillon have had the chance to switch guns out in the woods? Why should he have wanted to switch them?

It was true enough, of course, that there might have been time to fire two shots from the rifle. But to lay it aside after his first shot, for some absolutely incomprehensible reason, to take up another weapon, and to find Le Tendre still calmly puffing away at his cigarette in that window . . . No. It could never have happened in such a fashion; no time. So if a second shot had been fired last night; if it could be proved that Number Two had been the other man in that room; and if it could also be proved that he and Frenchy had had a violent quarrel about something . . .

If, if, if, Dillon told himself, and a bit desperately; quite a string of them. He would soon know, however. They had already passed the big dairy farm, and were approaching the last turn before Frenchy Le Tendre's house.

"Now take it a little easy," he cautioned Rita. "I want you to turn into that lane up ahead, and park there. Then nobody can see you from the road. All right now. Pull in under those trees, Rita. Swell."

He got out of the car at that point, and so did Rita.

"I'll cut over through the woods," he told her. "Just two minutes, Rita."

"I'll keep praying," she whispered. "Can you walk all right?"

"Fine," he lied to her, not wanting anyone at all with him, not even Rita, until he knew the full truth about Frenchy Le Tendre's whiskey bottle. "Doesn't bother me a damned bit any more. Wait in the car."

Then he edged off, attempting to walk normally for her benefit, and somehow managing it until he had the first cover of trees behind him. After that he hopped along with quick, clumsy steps. When the knee hurt him too much he rested against a tree or a big rock, and used the pause to check his direction by the tall line of utility poles out on Forestville Road.

In that way he was able to make a direct line for the Le Tendre house. Now everything around appeared to him either ink black or snow white, a strange, frozen world; but not a sound anywhere. The stars glittered beyond number, like a coating of thick frost over the sky, tree shadows tangled themselves on the snow, the intense cold had an almost dazzling effect on him, the knee throbbed; yet there was something of much greater moment than physical pain. So he hobbled on quickly, and sooner than expected was able to glimpse the side of the Le Tendre house before him—three black windows in a row, the roof gutter over them frozen solidly to a round crystal tunnel, and the roof itself pointed and glittering, with the shadow of the brick chimney slanted down across it, under the savage, bitter brilliance of stars and sky.

There were no lights visible in the house. There were no cars in the driveway. But most surely, he had promised himself, none of Rutherfurd's men would be still present at this hour. For what reason? And the next moment he could see that even Frenchy Le Tendre's wife had not returned yet for the funeral, because the dim outline of an official police warning against all trespassers had been tacked up in the middle of the front door. The house, then, was exactly as he had wanted it, and entirely deserted. He hobbled onto the porch, and got the flashlight out of his pocket.

Then on the nearest window to him, the one through which he had watched Frenchy Le Tendre pointing his finger last night at that other man, he saw that the storm sash had been cracked apart into long, jagged slivers of loose glass. Inside, on the house window, only one of the small individual panes had been broken, and someone had stuffed a rag into it, to keep the cold out. He got the flash turned on. After that he did a rather childlike thing. Before actually moving ahead to the window, he crossed himself in as blind and shaky a manner as had Sister Mary Frances back in the school hall this morning. Dillon the murderer now, or Dillon the fool. Which was he?

His heart pumped. Now he could see the armchair again, exactly as last night, the table, the ashtray on it, even Frenchy's drinking glass—but no whiskey bottle. Yet, if he had done what he wanted last night, there should be a few shreds and scraps of glass scattered around under the end table. Were there? No—or at least they could not be seen from his position out on the porch. The rug was a dark mulberry color, and he could see no whiskey stain on it, if there was a stain. He could see no jagged edges glittering against his flashlight, either. No glass.

He controlled thick, clammy nausea in him. No glass at all? But Rutherfurd could have swept up in here. Of course. He would have. Men would have been in and out of this room all day, and a lot of broken glass under their feet would have been an intolerable nuisance to them. Easy on, yet. He had hit the window just about where he had intended to hit it; he was not sure whether or not he had hit the whiskey bottle; but certainly, if he had, his bullet must have smashed on into the living room wall opposite. What did that show?

It showed the same details it had shown him last night, and in the same order, apparently. A cluster of three pictures, much too high for his bullet to have hit anywhere near, and then, directly underneath, the bookcase with its two big encyclopedias still on top, and the daintily posed China shepherdess still holding her skirts a bit up and out to each side. He saw everything but the one detail he wanted so desperately to see. It was a white plaster wall, with not the hint of a mark or scratch anywhere. There was no bullet hole.

The nausea deepened in him. No bullet hole? Pressing himself in as close as possible to the storm window, he covered every inch of the wall with his flashlight, but again fruitlessly. Then what else could he have hit in this room? The armchair, perhaps? It would have been an impossibly bad shot for Dillon the sharp-shooter, even at ten times the distance, and yet it was quite obviously the only hope that remained for him now. He had hit the armchair, or else he had hit Frenchy Le Tendre. What else?

He glanced back of him at the road, not remember-ing a moment afterward whatever he might have seen out there, and inserted one hand through the great, jag-ged hole in the storm window. In that way he was able to unlatch the hook. Then he knelt down, pushed the rag out of the hole in the outer window, slid his arm in as far as possible through that and at last managed to twist the inside window lock open.

It was more agony getting in over the sill with his bad knee, after foolishly kneeling on it, but he man-aged. Once inside he closed the window behind him, stuffed the rag back in the hole and examined the arm-chair. But the yellow and blue slipcover had not been penetrated at any point; the cushions, the sides and the back were whole; and there was no betraying fresh gouge in the wood edging on either arm, or up on top. Then at last he understood the answer waiting for him. Only one thing had been removed from this room today—Frenchy Le Tendre's dead body. It was the one thing that Sharpshooter Dillon could possibly have hit last night.

It seemed to him that he felt very much relieved by this last certainty; a bit light-headed, in fact. Fine, then. Very good. This morning he might have been forced to announce himself as Dillon the murderer to Sister Mary Frances, but nothing in God's world was ever going to make him do that with Rita. He had managed it pretty well, insisting on coming over here by himself; and now he would have to manage the rest of it, too. Rutherfurd and the state trooper should have done him the favor this morning; much better that way. But they had not, and so he would have to do it for himself right here in the same room, and right here in the same chair, if he wanted to. Fitting enough, then. Did the idea frighten him?

He decided that it might, if he stood thinking and thinking about it. Better not waste any more time, then. His bullet had broken the storm window and the inner one; it had entered the room; and it could only have hit Frenchy Le Tendre in here. Q.E.D., therefore. He knew where his bullet was, his one bullet; where it had to be. It was exactly where the dark brother had placed it. Dillon the murderer . . .

Yet he made one last try even then; the last of the last, he promised himself. Moving over to the window once more, he tried to line himself up with his position out in the woods last night. From that point he played the flashlight straight ahead. And then he saw that something had been moved in this room after all, if not taken from it. His flashlight, following the path his bullet must have taken, had come to rest between the two big encyclopedias on top of the bookcase.

Between them, Dillon thought, still oddly tranquil; between them. But last night, if he remembered correctly, they had been neatly stacked one on top of the other. Now they were separated by at least two full inches, and the one on the right hung out a little over the bookcase edge. Would Rutherfurd have moved them? Hardly. Two old encyclopedias? But if a rifle bullet had smashed dead center into the neck of that whiskey bottle; if it had sailed straight on for the living room wall; if it had hit the leather back of the top encyclopedia, and whipped it around; if the encyclopedia had been forced out then, on the rebound, to hang just a little over the bookcase edge as Detective Dillon could see it hanging now . . .

He felt thick sweat on him; the ifs again. What was Mamma's old saying about people who wanted too much out of life, and who expected only fine, pleasant things to happen to them? "If ifs and buts," he remembered, "were apples and nuts, oh, Lord, what great fun, to fill up our guts."

He remained crouched. Yes, indeed. If ifs and buts . . . But at last he got up, airy briskness in him, not at all believing the thing, not that crazy, and walked over to the bookcase. Then he spun around the encyclopedia on the left, saw what the back looked like and closed his eyes. A few thick tears showed themselves under his lids; Dillon the baby now. But then quite calmly and steadily he opened up the book, and saw a neat, crinkled tunnel of white paper inside. It was a thick old encyclopedia, ten or twelve inches through, and the paper tunnel had penetrated about halfway back from the point of entry. So in another moment, in his own hand, John Patrick Dillon was able to hold his own rifle bullet. Not until then could he believe the thing; or not even then. He had to sit down.

When he could stop the shaking at last, and keep his teeth from clicking rhythmically together, time after time, he got up without touching anything else in the room and walked out of Frenchy Le Tendre's house by the front door. Two or three minutes later, when he got back to the car, he found Rita waiting for him.

But all he did was to hold out the rifle bullet to her, and then, not wanting to be Dillon the baby a second time, and for Rita now, to draw her in very close against him. There was an idea for Detective Dillon then that never before had he held Rita in quite this manner; that never before had he been able to appreciate everything that Rita meant to him. Then he tried to explain to her about hitting the encyclopedia last night, and not Frenchy; but he had not quite finished about that when he heard the car.

It was back along the lane from them, not coming from the direction of town, or from the Forestville Road. Presently there was a dim glow of light over the winter woods that advanced slowly and carefully almost to the turn facing them, and snapped off there. Very shy and furtive those headlights seemed to Detective Dillon; not Rutherfurd, then. Who? But before he could make up his mind in regard to that he heard a car door open and close, also in a sly, furtive manner, and then a soft rush of steps behind him toward the Le Tendre house.

He had gestured at Rita to remain quiet and motionless beside the car. They listened again. They heard the footsteps moving away, farther and farther away; then nothing.

"But who is it?" Rita whispered to him. "I'm frightened, Johnny."

"I don't know," he whispered back; yet it seemed to him that he could have made a pretty good guess about it. "Wait a minute. Just stay right where you are, Rita."

He limped ahead for the turn then, trying to be as quiet as possible on his side, and slipped the service revolver out of his pocket. There was a stand of pine near the lane at that point, and he edged in until he could see the car on the other end. It had been pulled in under heavy shadow there, but he saw at once that it was the car he had expected it to be—a gray Cadillac. Then better and better, Detective Dillon told himself. The log jam appeared to have broken at last here, and with a vengeance; now everything was rushing out at him in full flood.

He went back to Rita.

"I want you to listen to me," he began quietly. "Don't get excited, Rita. You'll have to run back to that dairy farm down the road, and call Rutherfurd. You can make it a hell of a lot faster than I could. He can't hear you or see you, either. He's up at Le Tendre's now. It's Roy Vinson. I know his car, Rita. I think we've got him."

"Then I don't intend to leave you alone," she declared anxiously. "Not with him. You might—"

But he turned her around without arguing about it, and began limping with her for the Forestville Road.

"Do you think I'm crazy?" he whispered back. "Now I wouldn't touch a hair on his head, Rita. He's my insurance policy. Listen to me. When he gets back from Le Tendre's, I want Rutherfurd waiting right at his own car for him. Then he'll have to explain a hell of a lot of things for himself, and he can't. What is he doing up in Frenchy's house, for instance? Why did he sneak out on the men guarding him at the hotel? Why did he hide his car off the road? He'll condemn himself, I tell you. I won't even have to open my mouth about him, if he's still up in the house when Rutherfurd gets here. We'll have him right in our hands for what he did. Now I know who was the other man in that room last night. He was. Don't you see, Rita?"

"I'm not sure," she said, still hesitating uncertainly. "But what does he want here? Why did he come, Johnny?"

He showed her the rifle bullet.

"For this," he told her. "What else? He was in too much of a hurry to think about it last night, and all day today Frank Rutherfurd has had him under police guard. He was sewed up just as much as I was. Worked out real nice, didn't it? But don't stand here wasting any more time. He might be back soon. Do what I told you to do now. Get Frank Rutherfurd."

He started her along the Forestville Road, and watched her until she was out of sight from the lane. Maybe there had been no time to explain to Rita, he was telling himself, but now Detective Dillon was one hundred per cent sure of the whole thing. Somehow or other Number Two had managed to slip away from the hotel tonight, and had come right out here to Le Tendre's. And why? Because he knew that the second bullet, Dillon's bullet, had not been found yet. He could have put a few casual questions to Rutherfurd or Jerry Brenner, perhaps, as an interested and concerned party; but he had not been interested and concerned for the reason they thought. That second bullet, he must have realized sometime today, was vitally important. If it was found in Frenchy Le Tendre's living room later on, as it would have to be found, there might be a few uncomfortable questions raised. But if, on the other hand, Number Two got hold of the bullet himself, and disposed of it, then Dillon could tell any story he wanted to tell. There would be no factual evidence. Number Two would once more have proved out that charmed life of his.

Of course the perfect ending would be for Frank Rutherfurd to catch Number Two right in the house. That was a question of time, however. If Rutherfurd did not get here soon enough, then Number Two would have to be detained at the car. But detained in what way? If physical compulsion was used, then he would probably declare to Rutherfurd that physical compulsion had been employed to get him out here. It would be better, then, for Dillon to stay completely out of sight for the moment. Number Two's distributor wires could be ripped loose, or his keys taken, if he had been careless enough to leave them in the ignition switch; anything at all, Dillon had begun urging himself, but keep him here.

So he limped ahead even more quickly, and found the keys waiting for him—but found the man, also. The man had crouched down between the front seat of the Cadillac and the dashboard. The car was occupied, and Dillon could soon see who occupied it. Once more, as on that night last summer in Mountainview Park, the automatic dome light came on when he yanked open the front door, and then at last he found himself face to face with Number Two in grim fact; the end of the road for them.

Fortunately enough, he still had the service revolver in his right hand. He presented it.

"Now I'd watch it," he ordered breathlessly. "You see the gun? Who's with you? Who went up to the house for you, Vinson? Get out of that car!"

But Number Two remained calm and composed even at the direct order; icily calm. Not a muscle in his face quivered; not an eyelash moved. He continued to study Detective Dillon's left kneecap, with a quiet and remote look, as though speculating thoughtfully—his head cocked to the side, his knees bent, one arm lying on them, and one arm on the seat. It was such a very odd pose in Number Two, and such an odd, waxy look on his face, that Dillon became a little flustered despite himself. He stepped back, leaving the door still open and the dome light still on.

He heard the shot then. It was the first shot, and it missed him. There was a second. That one spun him around into the Cadillac door before he felt any other effect from it, and his bad knee gave way. He was knocked down, dropping the service revolver, and his head was snapped back into the ground that was frozen hard as a stone under him.

The solid earth undulated for him. He floated down and then up, and all at once he could hear a lot of people talking nearby—Sister Mary Frances, Rita, Frank

Rutherfurd, old John, Charley Dooley. There was something that Dillon wanted to explain to them, but Sister Mary Frances turned herself away coldly and scornfully; Rita gave him a look of hatred and loathing; old John threatened him with a clenched fist; and Charley Dooley offered the wise, chipper grin. "You and me," Dooley whispered to him. "What a hell of a combination, hah? You and me, kid."

But things began to clear up after a time. When they did, Number Two was still present, and the dome light in the Cadillac was still on. And Number Two was at last moving; not quite getting up, however. It seemed to Dillon that he was toppling out further and further from the car, still with no expression of any kind, until he had toppled out far enough to float down very slowly at Dillon.

Then that right arm of his struck Dillon across the face, and again dazed him. Yet it was not like a deliberate blow from a human arm, however forceful. There was something clublike and unyielding about it, solid as concrete, rigid as tough rock. He rolled away from Dillon after hitting him in that fashion, rolled over into the snow still in the crouched position of a trained acrobat, and came to rest. But his eyes remained open, and his knees bent. He uttered no word.

There was one other detail about him. A coating as of thin, grayish wax, polished to hard luster, covered the cheeks and the brown hair, the mouth and nose, the wide open gray eyes. A statue? Then a white marble one, Dillon told himself, and protected on every visible part with the greatest cunning.

All the other people became a little disturbed about Number Two. They moved away, whispering about him in hushed, sibilant tones, and became quiet. Only Poor Old Charley remained, the dark, freckled face distractingly close to Dillon, the brows crinkled together, the mouth twitching nervously. He appeared to be shaking Dillon, and speaking to him. He wanted to help, Dillon thought; the only one.

At last he got Dillon up against the side of the Cadillac, and left him there.

"You," Dillon got out at last, the idea perfectly clear to him, but the articulation a bit slurred. "Dark brother. You."

"What?" Dooley said. He glanced back at the Forestville Road, very anxious about something, with Dillon's hunting rifle under his left arm. Then he touched the statue with the tip of his shoe, and it rolled over obediently for him, and rolled back. Dooley uttered a short, cackling laugh, and pointed down at it.

"Look at him," he whispered to Dillon. "You ever hear the expression stiff as a mackerel, Johnny? Look at him. Holy God! He's frozen like iron, kid. I could hardly push him out of the car. Thought I'd have to break the seat first. Honest."

No statue, Detective Dillon was beginning to realize then; and no charmed life, after all, for Number Two. The wax on him was not wax, but thick, grayish-white frost. From under it, in an attitude of the most aloof detachment from them, and yet altogether horribly, Number Two continued to gaze up at all those remote heavenly constellations over the car. One arm continued to reach up toward them, but apparently with no strain or effort on his part. He was balanced delicately, in that accomplished tumbler's position, on the curve of his back. He ignored the both of them.

Then Dooley, shifting the rifle over to his other arm, again cackled. It was probably a nervous reaction. The dark, sad eyes watched Dillon with a dumbly haunted look of appeal behind them, as if for consolation or help. The Dooley grin flickered and jumped.

"Called me a filthy little cur," Poor Old Charley

whispered, at the same time nodding his head seriously as if to impress Dillon with all the overwhelming importance of that statement. "Started coming for me, kid. Well, he ain't coming for me any more, is he? But how do you feel? You're hit bad, Johnny; bleeding like a stuck pig. Why the hell did you have to come out here tonight? I never wanted to do anything like this to you. Why didn't you go straight to the hotel, like I heard you and the girl whispering about?"

And of course a certain adjustment had to be made by Detective Dillon now, after a beginning of that kind with Poor Old Charley. Something was not clear yet. Unless, of course, there had been two men in that room last night with Frenchy Le Tendre, and not one. But it would not be required to put any direct questions. They all reached a point, Dillon was able to remember, even though the ground still appeared to be rippling and waving under him; and then the pressure had to spill out. There was always a compulsion to explain what they had said and done, and what the other parties had said and done, as if a full understanding could be attained in that manner, no silly blame attached, and everything understood as they wanted it to be. So now Dooley, squatting down in a quick, cringing pose on the other side of that marble statue, dropped the rifle out of his hand, and reached over toward Dillon with both palms.

"But who can you trust?" he demanded anxiously. "Some great people around, hah? I thought up the whole thing for them, Johnny. I showed them how easy it was, and I set the price, even—five thousand for me, and five thousand for that lousy Frenchman. So the other guy hands over two thousand apiece last week, earnest money, and we were supposed to get the rest last night. That's why we met out here, all three of us.

"What do you think happened, though? You'd never guess, kid. He has the nerve to come around with three thousand on him, and that's all. Hell with us, he says. That's enough. He can't get any more. He even mortgaged his car to a finance company. Then all right, I says. Tell your old lady. Ask her. That ain't no problem. That was when he called me a filthy little cur, Johnny, after all I did for him, and while we're still arguing Frenchy grabs up the whole three thousand. Okay, he says. He got his, anyway. Now Vinson and me would have to settle what I got. But was that fair, Johnny? Was that right? Just tell me. Why should I wait like a damned fool and never get another cent out of it? Why couldn't the Frenchman have been a decent guy and split it with me, the way we agreed? I didn't want anything else from them. But they had to push me around, see? What the hell was I? That's what they figured. Poor Old Charley, that's all. Screw him."

And now all this was being poured out at Dillon in a whispered but still passionately indignant outburst; a man wronged. From the other side of the marble statue Poor Old Charley appealed almost tearfully about it, voice trembling, rifle forgotten for the moment, but very convenient.

Dillon propped himself up a bit higher. He had been hit in the back, he began to realize, and perhaps seriously; a lot of blood under his shirt. But that was not the important thing. Did he have any kind of a chance now with Poor Old Charley? He tried to estimate.

How long would it take Rita to get back to the dairy farm? How long would it take Rutherfurd to drive out here after her phone call? It was possible she had heard the shots, or it was possible that she had been in the house then, the doors and windows all closed. But at any rate there was no car to be heard yet on the Forestville Road, or off in the direction of town, either. He tried to steady himself. The one useful idea that came to him was to keep the conversation going between them as long as possible. He did not think that it would be too difficult for him to manage that. They had to get it all out of them, once they started. The problem was to shut them up, actually. He shifted a little, bracing himself against the car fender with his right arm.

"I only aimed for the whiskey bottle," he said. "All I wanted to do was to scare hell out of him, Charley. Did I hit it?"

"The whiskey bottle?" Dooley said. But it was off at a tangent from what mattered to him. He had to reflect nervously—rub a hand over his forehead, bite his lips.

"Well, yeah," he admitted finally. "I think you did. But you should have been there in the room with us, kid; like a Keystone comedy." He cackled a third time and had a hard job stopping himself afterward; but all the while those dark haunted eyes never shifted from Dillon.

"We begin knocking each other out of the way, Johnny, and yelling at each other, and then the Frenchman grabs his gun out of a drawer, and begins running from window to window with it like a crazy man. Well, he leaves the dough right on the table, he's so excited, and I figure I can slip it into my pocket and get the hell out, and let Vinson owe him then. All right. Only Frenchy catches me, because the other guy has the lamp on by this time, and tries to hit me with the gun, and I try to get it away from him, and it goes off, and I can swear to you that it could a hit me just as easy as it hit him. I never meant it, kid. Holy God! He looked like he'd got his head split open with a butcher's cleaver. I couldn't believe it. Split wide open, kid. Then I see the other guy coming at me, or just trying to get out of the house, maybe, and I'm so nervous and upset I keep shooting at him, too. And that's what happened. It was all over before I could even think, Johnny—both of them, and me standing there with Frenchy's gun in my hand, trying to realize it. You know how I felt?"

Yes, Detective Dillon found himself thinking then. He did know. He had been there himself, when the first news had come in last night about Frenchy Le Tendre. It was still the old team, apparently, even now—Dillon and Dooley. One who had meant the thing, and not done it, and one who had finished off Number One and then Number Two last night, in that mad complex of panic and greed in Frenchy Le Tendre's living room, without ever having meant it at all. Dillon and Dooley; only which of them, truly and honestly, was the dark brother?

It was a disturbing thought, a sick thought. He felt weaker and more nauseated suddenly; but again Poor Old Charley reached out for him in a desperate and beseeching manner.

"But you know I'm a right guy," he insisted again, in a shrill, breathless tone, as if that also had to be understood and agreed between them; very important. "When I'm treated right Johnny. You know that, don't you? Something came over me, that's all. I can't explain it to you. And you never got a feeling like that, kid? Never once?"

And Detective Dillon could not deny that, either. It was another point of full agreement between them. Yes, he had. The original motivation might have been a lot different; not the final result, however. It was indeed good actions to better, and bad to worse. But was he crazy thinking about stuff like that? He gritted his teeth. It had to be one or the other of them now—Dillon or Dooley. Where was his service revolver?

He remembered dropping it. But he could not remember Dooley picking it up, or showing it, and now it did not appear to be in either of Dooley's Mackinaw pockets; no sag in them. Then, turning his head slightly, he saw a faint silvery gleam way in under the back tire of the Cadillac behind him, and at once he cocked up his right knee between the tire and Dooley. Was it the revolver? If it was the revolver, could he reach it? It took great effort to push himself back a little, but he gained an inch or two in that way. Then he had to rest a moment.

"And after that?" he said. "After you realized, Charley? What did you do?"

"I don't know," Dooley whispered, this time glancing around fearfully at the woods behind them. "Hard to remember, kid. But you shot at him, so I figured you were going to believe that you killed him—only when they picked you up you were going to know damned well that you'd never killed the other guy. I had to think pretty fast, Johnny. See the spot I was on? So Vinson was lying on a little rug out in the hall, and I wrapped him up in it, not to leave any blood around, and dragged him out to his own car, and drove him to an old shed down the lane here, over on this side of Corey Pond.

"But I never had any idea that he was going to freeze up into a goddam chunk of ice, kid. I never thought about that," he insisted anxiously again. "What I hoped was that they wouldn't find him for a couple of months, anyway, and then it would be a lot too late to figure out what really happened. Or maybe they'd catch up with you in a couple of hours, and you'd try to shoot it out against them, and get yourself killed. Then I'd have been all right, of course. I won't lie to you, Johnny. I wanted it to happen like that. I had to protect myself."

Very weak, Dillon realized, and still bleeding a lot; but now that back wheel was only a little out of reach from him. And he had a minute or two yet, probably. Poor Old Charley would have to nerve himself up to finish the job with Detective Dillon. Keep him talking, then. He shifted over another inch.

"Then how did you get back to town?" he said. "Where was your truck, Charley?"

"Right there in the driveway," Dooley whispered. "I had to run all the way back through the woods from Corey Pond, kid, me and the one lung, but I made it all right. Then I decided that the best thing was probably to set up an alibi for myself, so I called the police station from Dewdrop's joint on Main Street, pretending like I'm the Frenchman, see, all hoarse and breathless, you know, because who wouldn't be, if a guy just pegged a shot at you through your own window? I even bought drinks for a couple of guys, so they'd remember me, and then I went out and met Jerry Brenner up at the hotel, and that was another pretty good break, the way I saw it. Who could figure I was responsible, if I ran inside and gave everybody the big news? You see, kid? I handled it all right, didn't I? Didn't I? What do you think, Johnny? Not too bad, hah?"

"Not bad at all," Detective Dillon said, but with quiet grimness. Now, it appeared, he had to pay Poor Old Charley a professional compliment. "Fine." He shifted again, and gained two inches; almost there. "But how did you get hold of my rifle? I never told you where it was, Charley. I never remember you asking even one question about it."

The sad eyes were peering nervously out at the Forestville Road now; the sad, sad eyes. But what could they matter to Chris Dillon's brother? Who the hell cared about them? They'd be sad, all right, when Detective Dillon could reach that service revolver. This was someone who had sold out a kid like Chris, or tried to, for a few miserable dollars. So soon now, very soon, and with all the justification in the world, John Patrick Dillon could really finish the thing—for Chris, for himself, for law and order, even, if he had to use that excuse. He could now touch the service revolver. With his left hand out as if bracing himself on that side, he began to edge it around slowly and noiselessly to him.

"No, no," Dooley said, the grin tired now, the eyes shifting for the first time to that marble statue between them still posed rigidly. "I couldn't, kid. I had to outfox you the whole way. That's why I lied to you the radio wouldn't work, and that the television set was out of order. I snuck out a tube when you were in the bathroom, see? Because of course I had to keep you under cover from Rutherfurd. The minute you got together with him, and told your story, there'd be a hell of a lot of details that wouldn't fit. Why do you think he came out to the station this morning? To ask me the last time I saw Frenchy, that's what. He knew how we'd been mixed up in a couple of things before, the two of us, and how friendly we were—so of course I had to swear to you that I hated Le Tendre, and he hated me. But then when I understood that all you wanted to know about was the roads— You hear anything, kid?"

"Not a sound," Detective Dillon said quietly. But he had. He had heard a car coming from town; Rutherfurd's car. "Don't get upset, Charley. So that's what it was. When I asked you to see if my car was okay, you figured I left the rifle in there, and you found it. Rutherfurd didn't have an idea in the world where my car was. And once you had the rifle, of course, you were all set. I thought you were pretty chipper when you came back from town this afternoon, and that was because you had the rifle, wasn't it? Then let them find the bullet. What would that prove? You had the rifle. Well, I have to hand it to you. You outfoxed me the whole way, and all the time I thought I was outfoxing you. You weren't even drunk tonight, were you?"

"Maybe a little," Dooley said, even the grin sad and

stiff this time. "Dutch courage, kid. It's a hell of a feeling to get. But that's why I kept the whiskey out in the
kitchen. You thought I was drinking it all, and I was
pouring half of it down the sink."

"Thanks for telling me," Detective Dillon said, and
presented the service revolver across his left thigh very
calmly. "And now let me finish the rest of the story for
you, Charley. Glad to oblige. Once you had the rifle,
you came back and told me Vinson was in the hotel, because you figured I'd make another try for him then.
Oh, you outfoxed me, all right—up until now. I'd go
down there after you pretended to go to sleep; you'd tip
them off the minute I left your place; and then they'd
put ten bullets in me as soon as I walked in. You'd even
let the girl take a chance like that. You knew she was
with me. And still . . . Well, you heard something,
Charley. You heard Rutherfurd's car. It just stopped at
the dairy farm back there. But he'll be here soon—and
I'll be waiting for him, too. You won't. Remember what
started this whole thing? Remember my kid sister last
summer?"

"Johnny," Poor Old Charley said. "Listen, Johnny. I
never meant—"

"Oh, I know," Dillon said. "You never meant. Okay.
I'll give you a hell of a lot better chance than you gave
her, Charley, and a hell of a lot better chance than you
gave me. I'll give you ten clear steps for yourself, any
direction you want. Go ahead now. Start running. You
might even make it, Charley—just the way I might
even have made it over to North Falls this morning.
Move!"

"Okay," Poor Old Charley said. The eyes flickered—
crafty, scared, cunning; the brain ticked. He became
anxiously persuasive, edging off as if without realizing
that he did, trying to get around the front end of the
car from Dillon. "Then go ahead, kid. Go ahead. You're

entitled. But I always liked you, Johnny. I mean that, and you always treated me like I was a pretty decent guy. That's what hurts now. I got a lot of respect for you, kid. You're all man. But the only thing I ever was . . . It took me a long time to see it, hah, Johnny? Funny thing. Poor Old Charley, all right. Let me stand up against the car, will you? I'm kind of scared."

The old snow job, Detective Dillon warned himself; the old sympathy pitch. And he didn't realize? He knew what Poor Old Charley intended to do, and he knew also that, shaky as Detective Dillon might be, he could place at least four shots in that small, cringing body before it could possibly get around the car from him. He was all ready. The dark brother, he told himself; the most miserable little son of a bitch . . . And yet, it came suddenly to him, still a brother, perhaps. They were the old incorporated firm of Dillon and Dooley, even now; the one who had done the thing, and the one who had intended to do it. And which was worse? as he had asked himself not too long ago in another connection. He waited another moment. Dooley waited another moment. Then Detective Dillon surprised himself very much.

"Give it up," Detective Dillon heard himself say, and in a quiet and very tired tone. "Give it up, Charley. It's no good. You don't know what it's like yet. You don't even suspect. Give it up, Charley."

But of course it was very difficult to reach them, enormously difficult. It had been very difficult to reach John Patrick Dillon. All at once, screaming down shrilly and hatingly at him, and then scuttling crabwise a-round the front end of the Cadillac, Poor Old Charley broke for the woods.

And he was permitted to break for them. Detective Dillon knew what the next hour or two were going to be like for Poor Old Charley. He did not envy him. He could remember what they had been like for Detective Dillon. So he fired his four shots in the air, to warn them back at the dairy farm. Then he rested himself against the Cadillac fender, in the heart of the great, glittering cold, in all the stillness, and waited for the police cruisers and Frank Rutherfurd.

CHAPTER *11*

They removed the bullet from Detective Dillon a bit later on that night back in the Hazard Lake General Hospital. Then they wheeled him off into a private room, still under local anesthesia, where he finally began to rediscover warmth and comfort for himself; very good things. It was about three o'clock Sunday afternoon when he woke up, and not long afterward Frank Rutherfurd opened the hall door and looked in at him.

"How's the back?" Rutherfurd wanted to know.

"They tell me all right," Dillon said. "Missed the lung."

"Well, then," Rutherfurd said. "He didn't get very far, in case you're interested. We picked him up trying to start that old truck of his near Corey Pond. So that's the credit side of the thing. You were shot down in trying to apprehend an armed fugitive. You took his gun away from him. You probably helped to prevent further bloodshed. Think they'll give you another commendation for it? You've got a pretty fine record so far, Johnny. I've checked up."

"Not exactly," Dillon said. "Everything considered. What's the debit side, Frank?"

"Ah," Rutherfurd said. He sat down next to Dillon, and unbuttoned that long, heavy overcoat of his. "There you're going to have a bit of a problem," he admitted. "I don't know what they're going to say about this in New York, Johnny. I can't promise you very much."

"I have an idea," Dillon said. "They'll think of something."

"Then hold up on it," Rutherfurd said. "For the moment. You remember Alex O'Neill, your old Chief Inspector down there? He's a friend and neighbor of mine now over on Birch Terrace; retired last year, as you probably know. Well, he's willing to help me dress up the report I send in, and his idea is that if we handle it cute enough you might get off with a temporary suspension from duty. You never know. He could have been tempted to do the same thing himself, Alex told me. In strict confidence, of course."

"Funny thing," Dillon remarked then, glancing out the window at the foot of his bed. There was a fine but somewhat clouded view out over the lake. Flurries of snow were again falling. "I believe I could do a better job for them now than I ever did, if they give me the chance. I have that feeling, Frank."

"Wouldn't doubt it," Rutherfurd agreed, eyeing him carefully. "Live and learn, Johnny. Most of them aren't a hell of a lot different from us, are they? It takes all of us a certain amount of time to find that out for ourselves. But you should have let me handle the thing in my own way, of course. I just thought Poor Old Charley might have a finger in the pie somewhere. He and Le Tendre were always thick as thieves up here. I even went out there yesterday morning to ask him a few questions."

"I even saw you," Dillon said. "From the school. And all along he kept insisting to me that he was the right guy, too. I just never had enough sense to believe him, Frank."

"Oh, he's a great Charley," Rutherfurd nodded. "Busy on one story before he finishes another. Last night it appears that he intended to drive Vinson and the Cadillac up into the woods back of St. Joseph's and leave them there. Then I suppose he'd have dropped Frenchy's gun on the seat, and you'd have had the two of them to your credit. But on the way over he remembered that he'd lost a glove Friday night, in all the excitement, and he decided to spend a minute or two looking around Frenchy's for it. I imagine he was in a pretty jumpy state by that time. He'd have fired at anything on two legs when he saw you back at the car."

"Poor Old Charley," Dillon said. He watched the snow falling. And perhaps, he thought, they wanted to reach over, too; to make contact. It was very difficult on both sides. How had he felt with Rita in the office last night? He had been there himself, all right. Now he knew.

He was still thinking about that when Rita came in, with a fine color from the bitter cold outside, snow on her coat. Rutherfurd got up.

"Then there's just one more thing," he said. "As a personal favor, Johnny. You don't mind?"

"Go ahead," Dillon said, watching Rita take off her things, and then touching hands with her. His heart ached a little, the first time in quite a while. He wanted it to. It felt very good to him. "Anything you like, Frank. What is it?"

"Oh, nothing much," Rutherfurd said. All the same, however, he appeared to be a bit grimly embarrassed about whatever it was, glancing down at the fur cap in his hands first, and then up at Dillon before making another and more successful effort.

"But I know it's around someplace," he insisted doggedly. "It would have to be. So where is it, Johnny? I'm conceding the thing. What in the hell did you ever manage to do in a town like this last Friday night with my new police cruiser?"